FORBIDDEN MAGIC

DARK FALLS ACADEMY BOOK 1

ANYA J COSGROVE

"Most of all, I hate you because I think of you. Often. It's disgusting, and I can't stop."
— Holly Black, The Cruel Prince

PROLOGUE

*B*eauty is vain. Beauty is dangerous. The kind of beauty I found at Dark Falls Academy is deadly.

I came here with a head full of dreams and an ironclad resolve to be the best mortal student the school had ever seen. It wasn't much of a stretch, since mortals used to be forbidden entry.

When I realized it was more of a battleground than a school, I started wearing shorts under my pleated skirt and wrapped chain mail around my heart. I did everything right…until I did everything wrong.

He bested me. He played the long game and bade his time, and I forgot we were playing a game.

That's on me.

Here I am, back on the same dark path I wandered my first day here—running. Not to class. Not from some creepy werewolf. This time, I'm running for my life.

I discovered his secret.

Deep burns pepper my red and black plaid skirt, and my thighs are tainted with charcoal streaks.

The tips of my toes curl around the edge of the cliff. A salty breeze bellows from the sea where dark waves crash against the rocks below, their stormy roils like thunderous applause to my demise.

I could jump, but he's got wings.

He prowls up the path toward me, his pale skin catching the moonlight. The uneven thumps in my chest terrify me more than the cold glint burning in his eyes.

Sickening tingles scatter across my neck, and his gaze softens for a split second. "Kneel, Fire Girl."

The coastal wind blows my hair forward. The long dark strands undulate like snakes at the edge of my vision as I lift my chin and seal my fate. "Never."

Despite my bravado, he's won. There's no fire left in me—I might have drawn my last breath.

I'm completely at his mercy.

FATHERLY WISDOM

"Got everything, Munchkin?" Dad asks from the bottom of the stairs. His gray hair sticks out in all directions.

"Yep. I'm ready." I haul my black leather suitcase down. The weight throws me off balance as I get to the entryway, but Dad catches my arm and steadies me. All of my earthly and unearthly possessions are in this bag. It's been enchanted to fit my needs, but the spell mostly only helped with space, not weight.

A soft grin blooms on my father's thin lips. "I don't know why I ask. You've been packed for a month."

I smile back and set the piece of luggage down next to my purse. "It's heavy."

"Copper cauldrons aren't exactly easy to carry."

He ushers me into the kitchen, where a fluffy pancake with cherry eyes and a banana smile waits for me, and my mouth waters. I perch on the chair, one leg folded beneath me.

Dad hands me the metal can of maple syrup before sitting next to me. "Well, since it's our last family breakfast until you lose all interest in your old dad, I figured we'd chat a bit. About what will be expected of you."

I press a hand to my mouth and swallow. "I know. No getting into trouble. No breaking the rules. This is a sensitive time for us witches, and I need to be worthy of the privilege. You made it your life's work to get us back into the Academy—I'm not about to ruin that for you by getting killed on my first day."

Dad's eyes darken. "Don't joke about that. Never talk lightly about your life, Munchkin. Especially around immortals."

I wrinkle my nose in atonement. "Sorry."

He pats my back. "You're going to do great. I bet your sister is beside herself with excitement."

My sister Allie left three months ago for Dark Falls, the most prestigious Academy of the three realms.

We both finished high school one year early, but I had to wait for my eighteenth birthday to start my supernatural education, and I've been counting the days—like literally tearing one day at a time off my calendar.

Allie and I were born three months apart. We're half-sisters, and while we feigned to be twins in the human world to avoid delicate conversations about how my Dad fathered two daughters so close together, we're both well-aware that it won't be easy to avoid gossip at the Academy. Dad represents the witches' and warlocks' interests on the High Council, the highest echelon of the supernatural government. When he disappeared for a year and came back with an infant girl in tow, it made the Witch's Tattletales front page. Allie's mom, a witch socialite, left him with his shame and two little girls to raise. Allie and I both made our peace with it and love each other like sisters should, but some of Dad's political adversaries are still using it in their campaigns against him.

Three months without Allie crushed my spirit. Being the one left behind royally sucked, but soon, everything will be right again.

There are no proper years at Dark Falls. Since so many students have different powers and limitations, everyone studies at his or her own pace until they're done with the mandatory curriculum and have enough credits to graduate. If your grades are not up to par, you get the boot. Since Allie only has three months on me, I figure we'll have several classes together. I took her advice and registered for five classes during my first quarter. I'm taking the three main subjects, Spells and Sorcery, Herbology, and History of Magic along with Divination—I've had a knack for accurately forecasting the weather ever since I was little—and Duel. Allie tried to talk me out of that one, but I don't want to waste any time. The human world doesn't allow for a lot of stray fire balls, so I need to practice my skills in a safe-ish environment.

"Are you leaving for Romania soon?" I funnel a chunk of pancake into my mouth.

"Tomorrow, but don't worry, I'll drop in on you girls at Christmas."

"Don't let them overwork you. And eat healthy, not just feasts and hotel junk," I say with my drill sergeant voice.

"Yes, Ma'am." He salutes me and wipes a few crumbs off the table. "Now, let your Dad impart a bit of his elderly wisdom."

I dump half a pint of milk in my big glass. "I'm all ears."

He's got that serious look on his face, the same one he had when he told me about boys and babies, and my cheeks immediately flare with heat.

"Dark Falls Academy is the best sorcery school in the realms for a reason. It represents our world the best. Thanks to years of hard work, there is no more elitist segregation, and all species have to live and grow together. Now, this doesn't mean everything is perfect, but it's an important step in keeping the harmony between all supernatural factions."

I raise a brow. "But...?"

"Most of the students went to Dark Falls Preparatory school. They have known each other for years and are used to mingling with other species. I fear I'm sending you girls off to a den of gnolls." He plays nervously with his cape, and the red fabric ripples behind him.

The last bite of pancake turns sour on my tongue. "Are you afraid I'll put my foot in my mouth and embarrass you?"

A stern scowl drags down his features. "I'm worried you'll barrel ahead with no concern for your safety. Some students have insidious powers, and half their parents are unscrupulous politicians. I want you to think carefully about which relationships you nurture." He rubs the arch of his brow. "Vampires got a bad rep. They're not as bloodthirsty as everyone thinks. Shifters share some qualities with their animal-self, so be wary of felines."

"I'll keep that in mind."

He clenches his fists. "Fae are the worst. Never make a deal with a Fae; you'll end up on your knees begging for your life. And never cross a mermaid. The ocean would never be safe for you again."

I nod in reassurance. "Don't trust Fae and play nice with the mermaids. Got it."

A dark cloud still hovers over his head. "And Munchkin? Don't lose yourself in the magic. Power is enticing, but it's a double-edged sword. The more power you have, the more people will want something from you. Don't play a game you know you can't win. We're writing history here, but sometimes, history repeats itself."

He's referring to the fact that mortals used to frequent the school. Dad was admitted in the '50s because my grandfather was a revered Magus—this realm's version of an Avenger, but with more dark magic and less colorful uniforms. About a year after Dad graduated, all the mortals at the Academy died in their sleep. The culprit was never caught. The investigators made it seem as though the students were responsible for their own deaths. How dare they soil such sacred grounds with their blood? The immortals assigned to the case brushed it off as a freak magical anomaly, and since then, mortals had been refused entry. Dad had tried to reopen the case after being elected to the High Council, but by then, all the leads had withered.

"I'll be careful, Dad. I promise."

He grazes my cheek with his thumb. "You're looking more and more like your mother, you know that?" He clears his throat, avoiding my inquisitive gaze.

He never talks about her. Never. I've learned to accept it. Why is he talking about her now? My mother was human. She never went to any supernatural school, and she was too poor to go to college.

"What has my mother got to do with school?" I ask.

Deep lines appear at the corners of his eyes, which glaze over for a moment—like he's not seeing me, but someone else.

"Nothing. Absolutely nothing. But seeing you grow up… it makes an old man reminisce." He claps his hands loudly, the sudden motion almost masking his deep sigh. "Now, let's get your stuff in the car."

3

THE DOTTED LINE

"*N*ame?" A sprite asks from the main desk. She's tiny. Her skin shimmers with tints of deep teal and midnight-blue, and her big eyes are coated in pixie dust. The luminous powder lights her face beautifully. She's three feet tall, max, but the stool she's sitting on puts us at eye-level. I'm not used to seeing Faerie folk, but I've seen sprites and pixies when Dad took me into work with him.

I try hard not to stare. My lack of familiarity with supernaturals shouldn't be noticed here.

The impressive lobby of the Academy's administrative offices sends my pulse flying, and my skin tingles in trepidation. The best sorcery school in all the realms is mine for the taking.

A big grin threatens to show on my face. "Jules Winslow."

I play with the hem of my pleated skirt. I'm not used to the uniform. My bare legs make me feel exposed—and a little sexy. I used to loathe uniforms. The ones at my old school were hideous; the skirts fell past the knee. This one's different. It comes in a few plaid patterns and colors. I chose our family's official design: red and black, with a tiny white stag embroidered in the corner of the big squares. The black blazer is both fashionable and comfortable.

The sprite passes her long, thin fingers over a leather-bound grimoire and hikes her big purple glasses up her pointy nose. "There's no Jules in my records."

"Julia. Julia Winslow."

The book opens by itself to a page near the end, and the tiny wings at the sprite's back twitch. "Here you are." Her eyes narrow. "Since you're mortal, I have to mark you."

"Mark me?"

"In case we need to find you. If something happens. Put your hand on the desk, please."

I begrudgingly obey. A throng of scratches on her desk display initials and names, and I run my fingers over the grooves where grime and dust gathered in the cracks. The names are seamlessly etched in the wood for centuries to come.

The sprite presses a stamp to the back of my hand, a burst of magic raising every hair on my arm to attention. Blue dye in the form of the school's crest—a raven with a feather in its talons—shimmers in and out of view, and I rub the prickly skin where the mark just vanished.

"Sign these." She hands me a stack of papers and a huge golden feather. It's at least a foot long and larger than my hand. The tip is pointy and narrow, each silky strand glittering with a warm yellow light.

I search the counter for a pot of ink but find none. "There's no ink."

"Mortals with no education. Next thing you know, they'll let humans enroll," she mutters—not quite under her breath.

I shift my weight to my heels and cross my arms. "Excuse me?"

Her irises morph into cruel slits, and her teeth bare in the imitation of a smile. "This is a blood feather, dear. You have to poke the tip inside your finger."

I follow her instructions eagerly despite her jab, curious to see what will happen. The golden tip sinks inside my index finger, and the whole feather sighs. It seems to drink from me. Blood rises up the center of the peculiar quill to the strands until the whole thing is red. A tiny streak of black in the middle part catches my eye, but the rude secretary taps her stack of papers again.

I concentrate on reading the—is it a contract?

Dad taught me that you should never sign your name without reading the fine print. This is not a contract, but a waiver. The Academy will not be deemed responsible for loss of property, loss of limbs, assault, accidental or otherwise violent death. The list goes on and on. It paints a colorful picture of all the imaginative ways I could meet my end.

That's reassuring as fuck.

Dad used magic at home, and I dabbled in a few minor enchantments and spells myself, but this is different. It's not just another new school. It's a brand new world with its own rules and many different types of magic and artifacts like a feather that drinks your blood and forces you to face your probable death. I read every word and scribble my name at the bottom of the last page.

The secretary seems to have forgotten all about me, so I drop the heavy waiver on her desk. She raises a file folder without sparing me a glance. "This is your schedule and the student handbook. We're still working out the kinks of mortal housing. You'll be assigned a room shortly. Just leave your stuff here for the time being and come back in an hour. Things should be sorted out by then."

I clear my throat. "I need to find my sister, Allie Winslow?"

She passes her bony hand over her ledger again. "Allison Winslow lives in Queen's Mab dorm. Take a left at the trident and go all the way toward the unending forest."

"Do you have a map?"

She grunts but hands me a sheet of paper.

I slip out, my sneakers squeaking on the freshly polished floors.

A year ago, this would have been impossible. Forbidden. For more than fifty years, no mortal has set foot in this place, but the insanity is over. We have as much right as immortals to be taught high-end spells and secret rituals. We have less time to put that knowledge to fruition, but that's good. Immortals are constantly wasting time since they have so much to spare.

I'm going to do great here, graduate, and find an awesome job like my father's—one that allows me to travel the world. I'll leave politics to my blue-blood sister. I want to go into paranormal investigations and kick some dark Magus' ass. Maybe even work for the Magisterium, the agency that governs all supernatural creatures on Earth.

Fire witches are a great asset in the fight against our world's most powerful monsters.

It'll be an honor to even apply for such a position, and it will all be possible because I'll receive the best education right here. I hop outside, energized, and find the trident.

The main path divides into three prongs not far from the main office, and I follow the left-hand side up a hill.

A blue colonial house with white shutters and a wrap-around porch stands in front of me.

Behind it, dark green trees gnarl into one another, their branches knitted together closely as though they are locked in a passionate embrace. Either that, or they're holding on for dear life.

Allie is sitting in a swing on the porch of the three-story house, and I pick up the pace. She inherited our father's light blond hair while I got my mother's dark coloring, but aside from that, we could be twins. We have the same small nose, baby face, and dark blue eyes. Her skirt displays the family's design, too, but with black knee-high socks and a matching V-neck tee. The loose hoodie hiding her frame is in stark contrast with the school's tight, red wool jacket I'm wearing.

I climb up the freshly-painted white stairs, and her eyes flick up from her book.

"Jules! You're not supposed to be here yet," she says, jumping to her feet.

"Allie!" I throw myself at my sister, wrap her up in a big hug, and squeeze. "I begged Dad to drive me up a day early."

She cranes her neck around like she's looking for something or someone. I jerk a glance behind me, but there's only us, and I didn't see a soul on my walk over here.

"You cut your hair," I say. "It looks great!"

Her usually long and luscious blond curls now fall right below her

11

chin. She extricates herself from my grasp and tugs on the ends. A few strands lick her shoulders.

Allie has always been obsessed with her long blond curls. It was one of the reasons we didn't share a room back home—the smell of hair spray makes me nauseous.

I let my arms fall at my sides. "Are you okay? You look a little pale."

The elation of being reunited fizzles out. She's lost weight. At least ten pounds by the looks of it, and she was thin to begin with.

She cracks a grin. "It's the exams is all. They're kicking my ass."

The knot of worry that had begun to spool in my chest eases.

Exams. On spells and dark creatures. I'll probably be the first to complain about them, but I almost wish I was the one with the pasty skin and dark circles under my eyes. Then I'd be a seasoned student rather than a newbie. At least, the term *freshman* isn't used at the Academy. I'm finally here!

The fabulous school my father can't shut up about, where I belong, instead of flipping burgers at Wendy's in a cloud of grease and constant teenage whining.

This is my destiny.

I hook my arm around my sister's elbow and pull her along. "Spill. What are the classes like? The teachers? The students?"

We weave up the round staircase to the third floor and follow a long empty corridor to the very back of the house.

"Classes are nice, teachers are either amazing or hateful, and as for the students…" Allie pulls down a folded staircase, and a puff of dust rises in the air.

The wood creaks on our way up the tiny steps. A black spider guards her web right at eye level, and I find myself staring at its hairy legs.

"You coming?" Allie asks from above.

I climb in after her. "You got the attic."

"It's cool, isn't it? I get to be alone," she says with a satisfied sigh.

The room stretches toward a lonely window in an awkward, semi-triangular shape. Allie's bed is tucked on one side, and her covers are in knots at the foot. A desk takes up the entire oposite wall. Books, papers, parchments, and ink pots clutter the work space.

I raise a brow. "Who are you and what have you done with my sister?"

Her nose wrinkles the way it does when she's annoyed. "If you'd arrived when you said you were going to, I would have had time to tidy up."

"You went from OCD queen to slob overnight?" I joke.

"I have no time to spare on stupid stuff now."

Allie describing her neat streak as *stupid* throws me for a loop. Her obsession for things to always be in the right place is another reason why we never shared a room.

The acrid smell of mold and jasmine clog my nose, and I grimace. A hint of freshly-cut lilacs also lurks behind the dusty smell.

The small alcove's round window gives a great view of the forest. Tall pines bristle in the afternoon wind.

I draw in a heavy breath. "I wonder where I'll be."

"Not here, I'm afraid. All the rooms are taken."

Things can't be as they were back home. I get that. But why doesn't she seem at all disappointed? How can my sister, the one who complains when she's alone for five minutes, relish this weird out-of-the way, lonesome bedroom?

I always imagined her being surrounded by fellow students, but she curls down on her pink bean bag chair, and she doesn't look at all inclined to go out again.

Her paper birds hang in mid-air over our heads. Since we were little, Allie has been adding to her intricate origami collection year after year. Most of the shapes are familiar. Others are new. A fiery phoenix towers in the middle of the room, flanked by a pristine white unicorn. A small, blue-winged butterfly sparkles with glitters. A black wolf prowls from the side. A dragon-shaped shadow hangs above her bed, while the slim angel with black wings sways from side to side. When we were young, she would hang them up with transparent threads. Now, she uses her magic to hold them there. They are arranged to catch the sun rays streaming through the window, and their bright colors warm up the whole attic.

My gaze lingers on the black paper wolf. "When do I get to meet this hot werewolf of yours?"

She wets her lips, her sight riveted on a textbook. "Um…I broke up with Jeremy."

My jaw falls to the floor. "What? When?"

"A few weeks ago." She casts the volume on her knees aside in favor of another.

"Why? I thought you were head over heels for him."

She waves dismissively. "We're young. We shouldn't tie ourselves down to the first boy who's interested."

The silence stretches into awkwardness. Something is off, and it has nothing to do with boys.

"I'm sorry to blow you off, but I have to prepare for my Mastery of Air final. The teacher got sick and extended the class to tomorrow, so I need to study," she says casually.

My mouth opens in barely-contained outrage. "Are you for real? You're not going to show me around?"

Her blue eyes narrow. "You should go to your dorm and prepare for tomorrow. Teachers are harder on us mortals, and we can't give them a reason to throw us out."

My sister is many things, but the perfect straight-A student, she aint. In fact, party girl would be on her list of flaws. I'm the responsible one, and I went skinny dipping after prom, so I bet she did worse. "What's wrong with you?" I'm trying to be understanding, but she's blowing me off. Like I can't possibly understand her predicament because I'm light years behind her. Like those last three months forged a crack between us where sibling pettiness and secrets took root.

She throws her head back against the bean bag chair and grips her hair. "I'm stressed out, Jules. We're outnumbered and underpowered, but somehow we have to do better than them to earn our place." She zips up her large hoodie. I notice the school's crest on the front. It must be part of the boy's uniform, and I wonder who it belongs to.

I pinch the bridge of my nose and take a deep breath. "I'll leave you to it then, but we'll have dinner later?"

"Sure. Let's meet in the dining room at five." She doesn't look up from her notes, and a sour taste fills my tongue.

JULIA WINSLOW'S SCHEDULE
DARK FALLS SATURNALIA QUARTER
MORTAL STUDENT

Monday
• 5:00am - 8:00am: Spells and Sorcery | Main Building
• 3:00pm - 5:00pm: History of Magic | Main Building
Tuesday
• 12:15pm: Mortal Seminar (3rd Tuesday) | Main Building
• 3:00pm - 5:00pm: Guided Studies | Library
Wednesday
• 5:00am - 8:00am: Duel and Applied Magic | Arena
• 3:00pm - 5:00pm: History of Magic | Main Building
Thursday
• 5:00am - 8:00am: Spells and Sorcery | Main Building
• 3:00pm - 5:00pm: Guided Studies | Library
• 7:00pm - 10:00pm: Divination | West Tower
Friday
• 10:00am - 12:00pm: Herbology | Summer Hall

4

———

SHARP FANGS

*W*ith a grunt, I clutch the parchment with my schedule and dorm number on it and haul my luggage behind me. The wheels screech on the stone pavement of the narrow pathway.

A warm wind breezes across my bare legs. The trees haven't lost their leaves in this section of the Academy, and the weather seems to match. I've been assigned to Summer Hall, a dorm that possesses a milder, sunnier climate than the rest of the Academy.

At the end of the path, a two-story Victorian home is nestled into the vegetation like a butterfly in its cocoon. Colorful orange strings of honeysuckle garnish the banisters of the wrap-around porch. The gabled roof is steep, and stained-glass windows hide the interior from passersby. A round tower with turrets stands cleanly on the right, but the house morphs into an amalgam of nooks of different shapes and materials on the left. It's like a crazy architect peppered in additional rooms at random.

I knock on the large green door.

"I won't let you gnomes cut my hair—" The door opens to a woman frantically waving a baseball bat about two inches from my face. "Oh." She calms down and rests the tip of the bat on the ground. "You're my second mortal. Welcome to Summer Hall."

The young woman's thick, white braid falls past her hips, swaying from her aborted home run. A pale green linen dress reveals an inch of her bare feet, and the flowy skirt gives her an ethereal look. "I'm Miss Eillis. I teach herbology."

Out of habit, I offer her my hand to shake, but she tugs on it and pulls it to her face palm up. Her fingers wrap around my wrist like vines. "Mm. Very interesting. Yes. You'll mesh in well here."

I bounce from one foot to the other, wondering if it's rude to punch a teacher for invading your personal space.

She lets go before I decide and motions me inside. "Come in. I'll show you to your room."

Plants grow everywhere inside the house. Pots and planters hold trees that stretch as high as the ceiling. Vines twist and weave around the ceiling's light fixtures. The fresh herbal scents are indistinguishable from one another—they're potent enough for my nose to wrinkle, and I bite back a cough.

"There are five dorm rooms here, each shared by two students. Six pixies live in the west wing, but they giggle so loudly that nobody can stand them. You'll room in the south tower with Lydia. Bailey and Blane live below you, but they're out right now. You'll meet them later."

An ornate round staircase full of red and orange flowers leads to the second floor. Miss Eillis opens the first door to a round room with many windows and two twin beds. To my extreme relief, there are no plants of any sort inside.

A stunning girl with luscious curves is laying down tarot cards by the bay window. Her flaming red hair sticks out in all directions.

Miss Eillis turns on her heels. "Well, I'll leave you girls to get acquainted."

My roommate stands. "I'm Lydia."

"Jules." I offer her a quick wave.

"You're a mortal."

It's the first time today that I've heard the word uttered with something other than disdain or apprehension, so I nod.

Lydia lets out a relieved breath and slumps back on her chair. "Thank the Gods! It's a nut-house in here. The two guys living below us are Basilisk shifters. As in snakes." A shiver passes through the girl. "How did you end up here?"

"My Dad is a Minister," I say.

Her brows hike up. "You're a witch? Nice! I'm a seer. My great grandmother was somewhat of a celebrity. That's why I got in. Honestly, I almost wish I hadn't. I've been here for six hours and still haven't found the courage to leave the room. That waiver fucked with my brain."

"You and me, both," I admit. My stomach grumbles. "Have you eaten? I'm starving. I skipped lunch."

"One of the snakes, Blane I think, told me the cafeteria is a bit of a hike. Of course, he meant that it was too far for *him* to walk if he woke up hungry at night, so he might have to eat *me* instead. He seemed to think mortals were the perfect bite-size snack. I'm used to people like us being the norm. Here, it's like we're lepers or something."

"Tell me about it. The blue dye thing—creepy."

"Right?"

We both nod enthusiastically, and my chest warms. I'm getting positive vibes from this girl, and I've learned to trust my witchy instincts.

Lydia and I follow the road leading to what is marked on the map as the dining room/gym/infirmary. We cross paths with a few groups of students and get a few whistles and catcalls, but no one stops to talk to us.

The building is modern and fancy-like. A steep black roof rests on floor-to-ceiling windows, and the glass allows a wide view of the well-lit interior.

We order the safest items on the menu—pizza and salad—and observe the other students. Three large banquet tables stretch the length of the cafeteria, and smaller tables are set in the corners. Most of them are empty, so Lydia and I sit across from each other at one end of one of the long tables.

As we eat, more and more students stream through the doors. I grab my phone and dial Allie's number.

Lydia raises her brows. "You brought your cell? The acceptance letter said that reception was spotty at best."

"Yeah. You can take a witch out of the human world..." The ringing tone gives way to a smothering silence. "Allie! Where are you? It's half past five."

A yawn stretches across the line. "Damn, Jules. I dozed off."

My eyes narrow. "Get your ass over here." Blowing me off before was rude. Not showing up now is unacceptable. We haven't seen each other in three months.

"I can't. I have three chapters to finish," she whines.

A burst of heat spurts from my heart to the tips of my hair. Lydia's eyes widen, and she glides her chair back several feet.

The orange and red hues of my fire magic lurk beneath the skin of my arms and chest. Curling my hands into fists, I force a deep breath down my windpipe. "Alright. Stay in your moldy room if you want." I jab the end button a few times and toss the phone on the table.

"She's not gonna show, eh?" Lydia says compassionately.

I comb my hair back and check that no one noticed my outburst. The last thing I need is to set something on fire on my first day. "It seems not."

"Hey, don't take it personally. I hear the teachers have been working the mortals hard. In hopes of proving that we're not worthy, you know?"

"That's bullshit."

Lydia smirks. "Preach it, girl."

"We'll show them. We'll show all of them how bad-ass mortals can be." I raise my lukewarm water.

"Amen." Lydia clanks her glass against mine, and a loud *clink* reverberates across the room.

The sound attracts the attention of a leather-clad girl sitting with her back to us at the closet banquet table. Brown curls dance around her heart-shaped face as she peels herself from her seat and prances over to us.

She flips a chair around, mounts it, and lets her arms hang from the back casually. "Newbies, hi! I'm Melanie Darkwood, the student body president."

The crimson lipstick spread evenly across her full lips contrasts nicely with her white skin. A teal bustier pushes her small breasts up, and five eclectic rings shine from her fingers—silver, gold, bronze, and a mix of the three. Her black, laced-up boots finish right below her knees. Somehow, this girl pulls off the dangerous biker-chick vampire look without looking raunchy.

"You're a vampire," Lydia says, startled.

Melanie flashes us a hint of her white fangs. "Thanks, Miss Obvious. And you guys are all everyone is talking about."

"Nice boots," I say with a grin.

"Thanks. I'm glad to see one of you Winslows has good taste."

I'm about to ask what the hell she means by that when a loud voice booms from behind her. "Juicy mortals!"

A big guy with his hair tied behind his head in a man bun strolls over to us. He's got the exact same coloring as our new vampire friend and the same nose. The swagger in his step evokes a blaring confidence, and his cute, boyish smile gives me half a mind to smile back. He's wearing a leather jacket over his uniform, and a dark thumb ring clashes with his skin.

Melanie rolls her eyes and waves dismissively in the other vampire's direction. "This is Trent, but ignore him. He's boring."

Trent puts a hand over his left breast and sprawls onto the bench behind me with his thighs opened wide. "You break my heart, sis."

Melanie examines me from head to toe. "So, you're Jack Winslow's scandalous second daughter."

I press my tongue to the roof of my mouth, embarrassed that my illegitimacy is already public knowledge. I'm living proof that my dad is not as lawful and honest as he wants to appear. While marriage has become mundane in some human circles, the highest ranked members of the supernatural political ladder are expected to conduct them-selves irreproachably.

"What about you, darling?" Melanie enunciates the word, and I catch a glimpse of her long, white fangs.

My roommate narrows her eyes. "I'm Lydia Hawks."

"The last descendant of the famous Viola Hawks, I presume."

"You presume right."

"Can you see my future now?" Trent leers at Lydia's generous chest.

My friend scowls. "It's not so bright from where I'm sitting. I see a lot of cold showers and disappointment."

Melanie snorts into her hand, and Trent flips Lydia off with a care-free smile, peels himself from the bench, and joins a group of a dozen boys in the back.

His sister leans in. "Newbies get a tour of the cliques. That's a new school rite of passage. Now, immortals don't like to be stared at so be discrete, but I'll give you the 411." She motions to the other end of the banquet table we're sitting at. About fifteen pixies are laughing animatedly, oblivious to their surroundings. "The pixies have a talent for sarcasm, but they mostly keep to themselves."

Melanie waves to the table next to us. About twenty students are eating happily, exchanging quips, throwing fries, or studying. "Those are my peeps. Shifters, vampires, mermaids, you name it. We vampires like to mingle. It's not much fun by ourselves. It lacks...flavor." She winks, and her gaze lingers a second too long on Lydia's neck. "Sprites are snub fucks, so they stay away from us." She flicks her hand like she's wiping the table full of sprite away from her peripheral vision.

I look around the room. "Not many witches."

"Not many mortals of any kind. You're outnumbered 30 to 1, my pretties." She chuckles. "You're like the school's scholarship students. The guinea pigs. If you survive the year, there will be more coming. If you don't..."

The taunt in her voice is barely enough to smother the spark of fear tucked deep in my chest. All citizens of this realm are categorized as human, but supernaturals can either be mortal, like witches and seers, or immortal.

Vampires age very slowly. Shifters and mermaids, too. As a witch, I'll probably die around 100 years old. That's great as far as non-supernatural humans go, but it's a far cry from the 600-800 years Melanie's got. Inhumans are Faerie folk and demons.

The vampire's chair screeches when she angles herself to the back of the room. "Trent and his goons are annoying but mostly harmless. The far-end table on the other hand..."

Lydia peeks over the sprites to the very back, and her cheeks heat up. "Who's that?"

I crane my neck around and catch a glimpse of the most beautiful man I've ever seen. He's got blond, almost translucent hair and an angular jaw. The redwood table he's sitting on emphasizes his golden skin. I wonder how I missed him before because his whole body radiates from within. The light coming off him pulls me in like he's the harbor and I've been forever lost at sea.

Melanie leans in conspiratorially. "The blond is Flynn Verinos. He's totally in love with his Fae-self."

My tongue drags against the roof of my mouth. "Fae?"

"Yep. We've got five representatives of Faerie gracing us with their annoyingly sinful presence."

Most of the Fae live their whole lives in Faerie. It's one of the three realms, along with ours and the demon dimension, a mysterious, hellish place full of violence and monsters. The Seelie court made a deal with the Magisterium a couple of centuries ago. The Fae have had a representative on the High Council ever since, and some choose to live in this realm.

Dad warned me they'd be here. He warned me they'd be beautiful.

He didn't warn me about how they'd make me *feel*.

The urge to run up to this Flynn and beg him to speak to me is almost undeniable. I want to memorize the exact shape of his lips when he smiles and drag my fingers in his luxurious hair. He moves like a cat, a panther, his large frame hunched against the wall at his back, his arm casually reaching up to the base of the painting hanging above him. The way he lounges is both nonchalant and perfectly studied, no movement wasted or unsure like he's posing for Michelangelo himself.

Melanie snaps her fingers in front of my face. "Damn it. I forgot how mortals react to Fae glamors, especially the first time."

Lydia jumps when Melanie slams her palm on the table.

Schooling my gaze back to Melanie, I swallow hard. "Are they as bad as people say?"

My father told me that the Fae lobbied the hardest against the Academy's new mortal policies. They can't stand that such inferior beings get educated in magic at all.

"Depends on your definition of bad," Melanie says. "They walk around like they own the place, and in a way, they do. We need the Fae's magic to keep humans from finding out about us now more than ever. Don't let them catch you staring. None of them would hesitate a second about milking their advantage over two girls like you. They might fuck you if you beg, but it's a game. I'm not saying it's not worth the hassle, but don't expect a call come Monday. You're only useful as a mirror to their perfection, and their egos are already too big for this school."

I struggle not to look at Flynn and fail. The door next to him opens wide, and a shadow obscures the mesmerizing Fae boy.

Holy Lucifer.

If Flynn looks like an angel, then the devil just walked in.

5

THE DEVIL PRINCE

*H*e's dark in every way Flynn is light. Black ringlets spill haphazardly over his forehead, absorbing the ambient light as if the river Styx had been poured directly into them. His jaw is chiseled, cut straight from a block of marble. The smooth skin of his neck gives way to broad shoulders hidden beneath the Academy's black undershirt. The knot in his tie, like everything else about him, is expertly disheveled.

His faded blue jeans hang low on his hips, standing out in a sea of black uniform pants, and I find myself staring at his ass.

Red-hot shame encircles my heart at the thoughts and images that follow—most of them R-rated, all of them inappropriate.

It's like I've gone from normal person to sex-crazed, desperate virgin in the blink of a very horny eye.

But the feelings are weirdly empty. His beauty makes me feel small and ugly.

The girl trailing behind him looks like a young, goddess-like Angelina Jolie. Her cheekbones are impossibly sharp, enough to slice a boy's heart. She whispers dirty secrets in the devil's ear, her crisp red lips curling. Her light blue hair is braided into a crown, showcasing her delicate pointy ears. Another Fae.

The boy's hand skims her butt, her short plaid skirt outrageous.

Lucifer sits next to Flynn. The girl sprawls on his thigh, and he holds her to him, one hand resting casually between her legs.

"That's Jessa Arabellameo. If you know what's good for you, you'll stay out of her way," Melanie warns, but I can barely hear her sultry voice above the ringing in my ears. "And the guy under her is our resident Fae prince, Cole Desirys."

Lydia turns green. "Did you say prince?"

Melanie's smile turns cold. "Yep. Hold on to your panties, mortals. We have a royal in the house."

Royal Fae are infamous for being irresistibly destructive. Wars were fought because they stole wives and husbands at will.

Cole angles his face to us like he heard his name, and his ardent amber stare collides directly with mine. It feels as though a ghoul ripped out my belly to play harp with my intestines.

He frowns and presses his lips to the girl's ear. She peeks over the rows of students to us.

A volcano of fire builds in my chest, and I fear I'll go Armageddon, so I push to my feet. "Excuse me."

I run outside through the exit opposite the Fae and run up the cliff. My breaths are quick and painful. My body shakes from the effort it takes to walk away from these forbidden creatures.

A salty wind whisks my hair up, and I follow a sandy path until the sea comes into view. The sun is setting over the horizon, the red, orange and pink melting into a midnight-blue sky. My heart is bleeding with colors, too.

My forehead is still feverish, but the barely-contained fire beneath my skin wanes in the cold night.

I can't believe I almost made a fool of myself and set the cafeteria on fire.

I clutch my necklace with one hand. It's an oval-shaped, natural emerald stone, and I mutter the incantation my father taught me when I was five to tame my unpredictable flames. Raindrops mist over my skin and soothe the ache.

My mouth is sour, and the bitter taste of my mortality taunts me.

Strong witches don't let themselves be bent by Fae magic. Not Winslows. Not me.

Glamors are a lie. They're nothing but a physical manifestation of their powers. It's an artifice, a vain attempt at bewitching weaker minds. Their beauty is tainted in that it is an artifice, a product of their corrupted DNA.

My dad fought against them for years, campaigning against their political ploys, pushing back at every turn to outlaw their wicked pranks against mortals. They used to abduct us at will, enslaving us in Faerie and herding us like cattle meant to satisfy their every whim.

They are the enemy.

When I'm sure my powers are responding to my commands, I drag my feet back down to the cafeteria.

Lydia is heading my way. "Are you okay, girl?"

"Yes. I had a bit of—"

"Hey, don't bother explaining. Melanie had to physically restrain me so I wouldn't introduce myself to him," she says kindly. "The effects will wear off. And salt apparently helps." She hands me a few packets.

Salt! Right. I dump three directly down my throat and gladly accept her unspoken offer to never talk again about the humiliating visceral reaction I just had. To a boy. A Fae boy.

My inner self snickers...*boy*? Every inch of him was alllll man.

I bite my tongue hard and wait for the annoying laughter in my head to end.

Lydia points to the dining hall. "Melanie invited us to stick around and get to know her friends."

I play with my necklace, the stone still hot between my fingers. Going back inside isn't safe. "I'm tired. I'll see you later."

Lydia rubs her brow. "Sure you don't want me to come back with you?"

"I'm perfectly fine." I wave goodbye and continue down the hill.

The sun has fallen beneath the earth, and stars are visible in the black sky. It gets dark fast here.

The trees grow in height and number the closer I get to my dorm.

Thick barren bushes flank the path until I reach the magical delimitation where the weather warms and the trees still flaunt their leaves. They form a beautiful arch above my head as I reach the Victorian house and skitter around the corner to check out the backyard.

The garden is splendid. Tall sunflowers stretch their stems to the sunless sky. Small herbs grow in planters near the porch. Green and purple vines sag, heavy with fruits, over a white gazebo. Big glittering flowers light a neon-bright path toward the very back where tiny phantom bonsais wave their skeletal hands. An array of vegetables wait to be harvested on the south side, and the whole lot is outlined by a thick hedge of electric-blue, fluorescent cedar.

The beauty of it all steals my breath away.

A tall silhouette bursts from the trail leading to the forest behind Summer Hall. The man's bright yellow eyes gleam in the night, and I take a step back.

Sweat gathers at the nape of my neck as he adjusts his trajectory and beelines directly for me. I dig my feet in the soft earth and hold my arms out in case I need to use my powers.

The boy stops a few feet short of the cedar hedge. He's got spiky black hair, the shape of a pro football player, and the predatory stare of a wolf. His thick arms are stretching tight the white Academy sport-shirt.

I tap my foot on the grass. "Who are you?"

He swipes his hand across his face, and the odd gesture betrays a hint of disappointment and confusion. "Jeremy Byers."

Jeremy...as in Allie's ex?

"I'm sorry...the scent. I thought you were..." His flustered face confirms my hunch.

"You thought I was my sister."

Understanding flashes in his eyes. "Yes."

I examine him with newfound interest. He checks all of Allie's boxes and then some. She used to go out with the quarterback of the football human team back in high school. "What's with the yellow eyes?"

He shrugs casually. "It's the full moon."

"I heard werewolves—"

He raises a hand in front of him in a halting motion. "That term is awfully offensive."

My cheeks burn at the blunder. "I'm sorry."

A cute grin tugs at his mouth, showing a hint of a dimple. "I'm just messing with you."

I brace my hands on my hips. "Okay, Mister Smarty-Fur. Are there many..."

"Wolf shifters," he says.

"—wolf shifters enrolled at this school?"

"Some. Most of us go to the Lunar Academy, but I prefer it here." Yellow eyes flash in the night.

The silence stretches and expands. Jeremy's intense gaze starts to crawl under my skin, and not in a good way. He steals glances at the house behind me like he's checking if we're alone...and I'm almost certain he's inching forward, the distance between us melting by the second.

I glide backwards. "I'll see you later I guess."

Jeremy grips my upper arm, suddenly inches away, and I reel at his swiftness.

My heart quickens at the sight of his claws, the long, black nails so pointy that they pierce my skin. The fire I cast away earlier rages to the surface. "Remove your dirty paws, wolf, or you'll be sorry." If he thinks he'll eat a piece of me tonight, he's gravely mistaken. I hope he likes his meat well-done, because I'm about to throw him a very special kind of barbecue.

A sickening scent of burnt fur pervades the air.

Jeremy cringes but holds on. "Allie broke things off mid-October, and at first I was fine with it, but then she *changed*. Something happened on Halloween. I found her after the party, and she was crying, but she wouldn't tell me what happened, and she wouldn't even speak to me after that. You need to get her to talk to me. You need—"

I free my hand with a swift twist of the wrist. "I don't need to do anything for you, wolf. Stop stalking my sister."

6

OMEN

offee is still working its way into my brain as I follow Lydia to our first class. It's five in the morning, and we rub sleep off our tired eyes. My hair sticks out from the bun I slept in.

There are four time slots at Dark Falls. The ridiculously early class from 5:00 am to 8:00 am, then 10:00 am to 12:00 pm, 3:00 pm to 5:00 pm, and the night class from 7:00 pm to 10:00 pm. Vampires and other night-time creatures have slots 2 and 3 off to sleep.

Spell and Sorcery is bound to be my favorite subject, and butterflies flutter in my stomach from excitement. My Monday and Thursday mornings will be spent learning the secrets of the best casters in the world.

The classroom is right above the auditorium, and it's the biggest one in the main hall. Twelve large wooden desks are set in three rows of four in front of a gigantic blackboard. Each desk has two stools.

Lydia and I sit next to the window in the middle row. I hold out my hand for a high five. "Hey there, lab partner."

She sets her cauldron and grimoire down on the wood and shakes her head. "Melanie told me this teacher picks the teams at random." She lowers her voice and shoots a glance at Bailey and Blane. The basilisk shifters are tormenting the white mouse in the vivarium at the back of the class. "If I end up with one the snake twins, I'll have to quit school."

The twins are tall and lean with pointy noses and jet black hair, but there's no question they pack serious muscles under their Academy jackets. When one of them steals a glance at my roommate and licks his lips, I shudder.

Lydia's gaze falls to my neck. "What's up with your hair?"

A few strands have turned bright red overnight, an aftermath of that whole almost-catching-on-fire incident. "It happens when I let myself burn a little too hot." I try to hide the red lock by combing it under the rest.

"You're a closet redhead," Lydia teases in a whisper.

"I wish. This is Santa-red, not normal-red." And I hate how it betrays my emotions.

Two pixies who live in our dorm come in—identical twins with long blond hair, bright blue eyes, perfectly applied pink eye shadow, and elaborate up-dos. They giggled at us this morning. Apparently, our disheveled appearances cracked them up to no end. I watch for my sister's arrival, but students stream in one by one until there are only two seats remaining, and Allie is still a no show. My heart skips a beat when Flynn waltzes in.

I hold my breath, and sure enough, the devil follows.

I force my gaze back to the front.

The teacher has smooth ebony skin and purple irises. Her hair is as black as mine and tied at the back of her neck, a jeweled spike holding it in place. A gray pencil skirt and matching jacket emphasize her generous curves, her hourglass shape so pronounced that I almost expect sand to fall to the floor as she paces the room.

The clock strikes five, and she opens her mouth. Complete silence falls over the class in an instant.

"For those of you who are joining us this quarter, I'm Rose Dever-aux. New blood means new spells and a lot of hard work to be done. I don't keep slackers in my class. I don't give extensions or second chances. This is the spine of your curriculum, and if you're skilled and motivated, we have years to get acquainted. If you graduate from my class, you'll be amongst the elite sorcerers of the world. But I warn you, only one in five students makes it to the end. One in five is kicked out of the Academy altogether."

She takes a sorcerer's hat from her desk and tugs at the pointy end. Dust sprinkles to the ground while she tucks a piece of parchment and a black feather inside. "We're going to let chance determine your partners. Newbies, don't be intimidated if you end up with one of our seasoned students. In fact, it will be a great opportunity for you to catch up."

She goes around the room to the other side and lets the students pick names from the raggedy hat. Groans and squeals resonate around me as the pairs form, until she reaches Flynn.

I cross my fingers between my thighs.

The ethereal blond Fae flicks a small piece of parchment open, and his wolfish stare zeroes in on Melanie. "Want a bite, Mel?"

"Been there. Done that." She struts in Flynn's direction.

The dark-haired prince relinquishes his seat to Mel and reaches for the hat.

There are only seven other students left.

Not me. Not me. Not me. Pick someone else. Anyone else.

I rest my elbow on the windowsill. The glass is cold against my skin.

SPLAT.

A dark mass crashed into the window. Letting out a surprised cry, I jerk away.

"That's an omen if I've ever seen one," Lydia grumbles.

The teacher opens the window out front and sticks her head out, looking down at the grounds. Smoker lines appear around her tight mouth, and she casts me a nasty glance like I'm somehow responsible for this.

Blood drips along the glass. The crimson trickle forms a B-shaped blotch. My nails rake the desk, and I press my necklace deep into my other palm. The voices around me blur into an unintelligible void.

"Julia? Julia Winslow," the teacher calls, now standing next to Cole.

I turn around.

Cole is waving around a piece of parchment with my name on it, and dread ties up my tongue. He skips over to me and shoos Lydia away with one dark glare. His feline grace makes my heart thump.

Dad's voice resonates in my head. *Never make a deal with a Fae; you'll end up on your knees begging for your life.*

My roommate lunges out of her chair and slithers to the back. I shoot her an accusing look.

Lydia shrugs like I can't possibly expect her to share my bad luck.

Flynn snickers. "Don't cough too hard, Cole, or you'll kill the mortal by accident."

Cole's lips quirk at his friend's bad joke, and my insides turn to mush. Fuck. Up-close, his pale skin gleams from within. His dark curls are longer on top than on the sides. The loose ringlets cast shadows over his angular features. It's the kind of face—the kind of man—that sparks unhealthy obsessions. Jealous glares tingle at the back of my neck as half the class seethes behind me—especially the Barbie twins.

I sink my nails into my palms to keep from touching him.

"I'm Cole." His voice is fucking unbelievable. It's got the raspy drawl of a rock star mixed with a crystal-clear pitch. It's secretive. Sexual.

My fight-or-flight instinct kicks in.

I glare at his outstretched hand and keep my arms firmly wrapped around my body. "I know who you are."

His brows raise, and his amber eyes grow a shade colder. A peculiar darkness passes over his face before he lets his rejected hand fall to his side. The bunch of his muscular forearms makes me gulp. His gaze skims me up and down and up again, his face stuck in a sneer like he finds me lacking in everything that counts. Like I'm a particle of dirt he might scrub off with one flick of his stupidly powerful hands. "Ditto, Sabrina." The words are frostier than a puff of breath in an icy desert.

I clear my throat and hold the intense stare. "My name is Jules."

With a shrug, he breaks the spell and sits on the stool next to mine.

The change in position makes him slightly less scary, but he's got a good foot on me.

The corner of his mouth twitches before he leans in.

I stretch away, almost jumping off my seat to keep a safe distance between us.

The satisfied grin on his face is worse than a punch. "You witches should watch yourselves. The school might have allowed mortals to come back, but not everyone agrees." His measured voice brims with quiet violence, a venom wrapped in such a rich, velvety packaging that it expects you to drink willingly from its sting.

It reeks of wealth and entitlement.

"Is that a threat?" I croak, unable to think of something better.

"I'm just saying. Don't go out alone at night, Sabrina." He winks and turns to his cauldron with a lazy smile.

A metallic glint catches my eye. Three round earrings—one brass, one copper, one silver—almost mask the ends of his pointy Fae ears.

Schooling my gaze back to the front once more, I watch the rest of the teams being made, but I can barely hear a word above the whooshing of blood at my temples. We have to practice time-delay modifiers to basic spells, essentially adding a timer on spells we're already comfortable with.

It'd be easy enough if I wasn't so on edge.

The Fae's proximity creates ripples of goosebumps across my arms. The heat of his thigh travels through the few inches of space between us like a beacon. My chest is too warm, and the tips of my fingers crackle with fire.

Deep breaths.

The unlucky draw ruined my favorite class before it started, but I can't afford to let him know how he affects me. Besides, the glamor will fade as I get use to his presence.

Only, I don't want to get used to Cole. My witch's instincts are screaming at me to run far, far away and never, ever look back.

7

FORTUNE

"*I* can't believe you ended up with Jeremy, and I have to sit beside that," I motion to Cole's retreating back, "for three whole months."

Lydia winces in commiseration.

An icy raindrop splashes on my nose, and I lean against the main building's wall, my jacket scratching along the brick. A puddle creeps closer and closer to my cute, but totally not waterproof, heeled boots. Class finished fifteen minutes ago, but we're waiting for the torrential rain to relent. We have the whole afternoon off until I need to be at History of Magic and Lydia at Guided Studies.

"What did he say to you? You look flustered." The purple rubber boots on her feet remind me of my mistake. The seer warned me about the rain, but I wanted to make a fashion statement.

I purse my lips together. "What didn't he say?"

"Did he flirt?" she asks quietly.

Why the hell would Lydia get that idea? "No. He mostly warned me of my impending doom."

"I heard they're going to initiate us tonight."

I roll my eyes.

The emergency exit next to us booms open, and Lydia jumps

closer to me. Melanie prances out and adjusts her skirt. Her hair is disheveled. When Flynn skips out behind her, closing his belt buckle, a fierce blush rises to my cheeks.

"Been there, done that twice, Mel." He smacks her ass playfully.

She spins around and pokes his chest with a very intimidating finger. "Don't let it go to your head, Tinker Bell."

Flynn growls and hooks his hand around her neck, pulling her to him.

He kisses her, and strong-willed, bloodthirsty Melanie melts under his touch. Her back arches in a silent moan. With her eyes closed and her head tilted back, she looks like Flynn's kiss is the only thing tethering her to this Earth.

Lydia and I gape.

"I can't look away," my friend whispers with a hint of shame.

"Me neither."

Melanie and Flynn are still devouring each other, Flynn's hand holding Melanie's ass flush against his crotch. A glow emanates from both of them as though Melanie's skin absorbed a bit of Flynn's Fae glamor.

"This is enlightening," Lydia adds.

My tongue sticks to the roof of my mouth. "Mm-mm."

"What the fuck is he doing to her?"

"No idea."

I sort of want to find out, but I smother the impulse with a healthy dose of disgust and judgment.

Flynn chuckles against Melanie's cheek and pushes away from her. "You know what the French say. Jamais deux sans trois..." His ardent gaze falls on Lydia, then etches into me.

I'm not sure what the French words mean, but it's a sexual innuendo of some kind.

It's like his blue eyes can read the forbidden fantasies punctuating our heavy breaths. "Get in line, mortals. I'm not above trying on one of you for size." His index goes from me to my roommate. "Eeny... meeny...miny..." With a gleeful salute, he spins around and hurries off the opposite way.

Lydia fans her neck dramatically with her hand. "His behavior is appalling, and yet…"

The heels of Melanie's knee-high boots splash into the puddle without hesitation, and she stops an inch short of us. "Can I count on you ladies to keep your mouths shut? I can't handle another lecture from Trent."

I make a zipping motion over my lips and blink away the heated images that are imprinted on my brain. The last thing I need is for my mind to associate Fae with sex more than it already does, but the two together are like oatmeal sticking to a burnt pot.

Melanie checks her skirt, the black and white plaid falling at her mid-thigh. "Can't believe I got him as a partner. He's going to torment me all quarter. You, you got lucky."

I assume she's talking to Lydia.

"Jeremy seems nice," my roommate admits.

Melanie purses her lips in disgust. "I wasn't talking about the wolf. I was talking to Winslow."

I scoff. "How did I get lucky?"

"Cole takes his grades seriously. Unlike…every other boy I know."

I consider her answer. If she's right, I won't have to do the whole project by myself, but it means I'll have to work with Cole.

Lydia frowns. "What's wrong with Jeremy?"

"Jeremy got expelled from Lunar Academy for tearing out his girl-friend's throat. I heard he caught him cheating on him and wolfed out. She barely made it to the hospital. Be careful, Red." The rain eases down to a drizzle, and Melanie hooks her arms in ours and pulls us along. "Your sister did herself a favor by breaking up with him."

The mention of Allie starts an itch on my neck. Despite this new information that Jeremy is a serious creep, the wolf was onto some-thing. Allie's been acting too weird. "Speaking about Allie, did some-thing happen to her? Maybe on Halloween?" I ask lightly. I don't want to come off as a paranoid freak.

Melanie shrugs. "Not that I recall. She had a great time at that party."

We cross Night Hall, the dorm dedicated to creatures who prefer to live in the dark. The absence of windows would make any house look bleak, but this one's got a definite coffin vibe, and a cold patch glides across my shoulders.

The fallen leaves at our feet crack under Melanie's boots. "Well, I'm overdue for a nap. See you ladies later."

Lydia and I return to Summer Hall. The cold rain gives way to a warm breeze, and we unbutton our jackets. What kind of magic can uphold a spell of this magnitude? I figure the whole faculty strengthens the weather-influencing spell regularly for it to be so damn strong.

As we near the wild vegetation, Miss Eillis' high-pitched voice erupts through the trees.

She's chasing gnomes in the garden, her long skirt drenched with mud. One of the brown, hunched creatures has got her gardening gloves in his gnarly hands. He waves them around to taunt her.

"You little thieves will find another garden to squat!" Miss Eillis roars. The sound shakes the earth, and her long white hair flows around her like it's alive.

The gnome grimaces and spins around to flash her. Engrossed in his victory dance, he fails to notice us arriving, and I snatch the gloves from his hand. The fucker bites my index finger, and I shake him off me with a yelp.

He scampers off before I can kick him, and I return the stolen gloves to my dorm supervisor.

"Thank you, Jules. You should sanitize that cut," Miss Eillis says.

A drop of blood pearls on the tip of my finger, the puncture wound already inflamed and itchy. "I'll wash it later."

"No need. Use this." She snaps a small, bean-shaped pink fruit from one of the bushes and hands it over.

"What is it?" I ask.

"Pink bean stalks. They'll seal a superficial wound in no time. You've never used one?"

I spurt the insides of the fruit on my wound. "I'm not much of a green thumb, I'm afraid."

The sun peeks from the morning clouds, the fog clearing by the minute. A trail of sweat drips down my back. It'll be warm today.

"This garden is just a dream," Lydia trails off with stars in her eyes.

Miss Eillis beams at the praise and motions to the big area we're in. "This section is for the students." She points to the patch of bushes, trees, and vegetables surrounded by a gold thread. "This one, however, is off-limits. These plants have been nurtured for decades to become the purest and most potent ingredients in the three realms. You need a permit to access them, and the High Council is very strict on who gets to use them. Don't poach, or you'll be expelled faster than a gnome can flip you off."

Lydia and I nod in understanding, and her eyes wander to the closest tree where red, plump, triangular fruits shine in the sunlight. "What are those?"

"That one is a bloody thorn bush, named after its thorn-shaped fruits."

I graze the crimson flesh, and my mouth waters at the sweet nectar scent lingering in the air.

"They look delicious, but they're actually wretched. They're used in antidotes and emetics." She points to a taller tree bursting with small berries. "These are edible. They're poppy currant buns. They'll help you relax before a stressful exam, but eat too much, and you'll sleep the day away."

Miss Eillis points out a few other plants and explains their uses and properties.

Lydia is fascinated. I struggle to keep up.

After digging out the last of the gnomes, we gather in the kitchen and prepare some tea. Miss Eillis even gets a cake from the fridge. "Now, I'm not supposed to feed the students, but you deserve a treat for helping me."

She serves us each a piece, and I sip on the cup of chamomile goodness. "Summer Hall is always in bloom, then?"

"We do have seasonal changes, otherwise we wouldn't get a harvest, but it's a mild fall and a short, milder winter. That's why they plan to send more and more mortals here." She averts her gaze.

I grit my teeth together. "Because they think we're weak?"

With a sheepish grin, she says, "Blane and Bailey would hibernate if they slept anywhere else on campus, so it's not strictly against you girls."

We chat for a bit, going over the basics of the Academy—both faculty and students—and I get the sense that Miss Eillis is a bit of an outsider herself. Maybe they didn't stick us here because of the warm weather. Maybe it's because the other supervisors gave the undesirables to her.

She combs her hair and braids it as we chat, and the strands undulate to a non-existent breeze. I still don't know what she is, but it's rude to ask.

She rises to her feet. "I'll leave you girls to it. Why don't you show Jules your beautiful tarot deck, Lydia?"

I raise my cup in the air. "Thanks, Miss Eillis. I had a great time."

When I'm sure she's out of earshot, I lean toward my roommate. "What is she?"

"No idea. She's powerful, though. I can feel her energy."

I make a mental list of every supernatural creature working at the Academy, but Miss Eillis doesn't fit into any category.

Lydia pries a wooden box from her bag and slides open the top. She shuffles the cards expertly. "Are you up for a reading? I could use the practice."

Witches know better than to laugh at a tarot deck, especially when a seer offers you a reading.

Ignorance is bliss, as they say, but I can't help but nod.

Lydia fans her deck across the table, the gesture easy and without thought. She retrieves a card and lays it straight in front of her.

A gorgeous woman with her arms stretched out is standing at the edge of a precipice. A white toga is draped around her curves, and doves spin a red thread around her chest as she gazes into the unknown.

I lean closer. "The Fool."

Lydia smiles. "Yes."

"Wow, I've never seen this deck before."

"It was my grandmother's. She painted all the images herself," Lydia says proudly. "A symbol for new beginnings and adventures, pleasure, passion, thoughtless, and rash behaviors."

Shivers lance up my spine, and I wiggle my shoulders, my mouth dry.

Lydia grazes the spread deck until her index finger twitches over a card. She presses on it and slides it out of the line.

"The Tower." She lays it across the Fool. "A sudden change, a crisis."

At the top of a big tree that looks a lot like a Sprite nest, a tower has just been split in two by a bolt of lightning. Fire rises from the rubble. The orange and red flames contrast against the stormy sky, and I hold my breath. The artistry of the piece is so raw that I feel as though I might actually be zapped if I touch it.

Lydia reaches for a third card and flips it over the other two. I instantly recognize it even though it's not one I'm used to.

A hoofed figure with large transparent wings is weaving a spider web between his wraith hands. A small heart is held captive in the net. The long, skeletal claws bring a chill to my bones, and I can't help but notice his pointy ears. The dark hook of the scythe curls over his head. Under the hill on which he stands, a naked, prostrate woman is holding her head, her wrists chained to the rock.

Lydia's voice trembles. "The Devil. Overindulgence, or choosing to stay in the dark."

My lids flutter. "Addiction and enslavement." Lust and desire...

Lydia's throat bobs, and she quickly squares the deck. "I'll do another reading tomorrow. I'm clearly off my game."

Our gazes meet, and the weight of what just happened passes between us. It's not about the reading, but the card itself.

The eyes, the face. The dark curl of the hook falling over his forehead. It's uncanny.

We're both too stunned and scared to admit out loud that the figure her great grand-mother painted a century ago looks like Cole Desirys.

8

HIDE AND SNEAK

*M*elanie claps her hands three times and uses them as a magical megaphone. Her voice thunders across the clearing. "The hide and seek monthly games are a Dark Falls Academy tradition. Newbies, for your initiation, we figured we'd add a certain level of difficulty. Magda, will you do the honors?"

About fifteen students stand with me in front of Melanie's pedestal. I stand on my tip-toes, wide-eyed, and search the crowd for Allie. Melanie had herded us into the clearing leading to the forest after the History of Magic class, and it's already pitch black outside.

A pixie with purple hair flies over us and sprinkles a bit of pixie dust. My skin starts to gleam like a reflective surface.

"Refuse to participate, and you'll automatically lose. Plus, we'll tie you up to these trees, naked." Melanie motions to a lonely patch of half-dead pines. "Is everyone clear on the rules? Now, as usual, the twenty best hiders from last month's games get to be seekers."

Brie, a mermaid shifter with long tanned legs and short, fluorescent lime hair, hops to her feet. "The first twenty found will split up all the students' chores for the month. Anything goes except for changing reality planes." The girl points directly to the very back of the crowd with a half smile. "Yes, I'm looking at you, Cole. No zapping to Faerie this time, or you forfeit."

I stare ahead while everyone else cranes their necks around to look at the prince's reaction.

"Oh, I almost forgot. Mortals have to wear protective gear." Melanie tosses ugly hockey-style helmets at us.

Olson Lewis, a cute warlock with an electric-blue punk haircut, shouts over the crowd. "What? Why?"

Melanie grimaces. "They threatened to shut the games down if we didn't."

With a somber frown, I clip the white helmet over my head and help Lydia with hers—the strap tangled in her hair.

Brie wets her lips and continues, "If a seeker touches you, a number will appear on your skin so you know in which order you were found. If you leave the forest before the horn signals the end, you'll automatically receive a blue number, and you don't want to find out what happens to quitters."

A wicked grin spreads on Melanie's mouth. "Now, you'll have a five minute lead. Use it wisely... Go!"

I've never been inside the forest before and follow Lydia's lead until we reach the trees.

"We should probably not stick together." She motions to the pixie dust that radiates off our skin.

"You're right. Good luck."

"It was nice knowing you," Lydia says with faux-drama before running straight east.

I turn west. A raven crows from a branch, its slick black feathers shining in the night. He lunges into the air, and I follow.

The lights of the seekers aren't visible anymore, and I tread deeper and deeper into the unending forest. The damn helmet is too big and keeps falling over my eyes, so I tuck it inside a hollow trunk. The flip side of the glittering dust is that it makes it easy to avoid holes and branches. The air is crisp and cool, and I glide between the trees. Pine needles and dead leaves rise in my wake.

If I can smell my own trail, it's a problem, so I pluck an oyster mushroom and a patch of lichen from a rotting trunk.

Dad took me hunting every year and taught me basic tracking spells. I cast a stink bomb with the makeshift ingredients, leave it on the ground, and run. When it goes off in a minute, it'll create a stench so potent that my subtle scent will be lost amongst the skeletons of trees.

There's a stream ahead. Cold water bites into my legs as I cross it. My progression toward the other bank is slow, and the water reaches my knees in the middle. A steep rock formation towers from the other side, and a slim silhouette rises from the glassy surface. "Get lost. This is my spot," a feminine voice barks.

Startled, I stagger up the river bed to solid ground.

The raven from before flaps its wings from a nearby tree. Two beady blue eyes shimmer in the night before it takes flight. Its dark wings bring a chill to my core, and I follow it to a crack in the rocks.

A loud voice booms from the dark. "I see a newbie over there! Come out, come out wherever you are!"

Branches snap and crack. My heart quickens as I slip inside the cavern, and the taunting voice is replaced by the steady dripping of water.

The stone pillars force me to slalom up a narrow path until I reach a dead end.

Fuck.

I'm stuck.

Ripe for the picking.

A silver twinkle catches my eyes, and a shadow moves in the darkness, about twelve feet above my head. I frown and consider the rock wall with new eyes. Someone is hiding up there.

I wrap a spider web around my hand, mutter a basic sticky spell under my breath and start climbing. I haul myself up with my hands and feet until I reach a natural alcove in the granite, its dark, narrow opening invisible from the ground.

A loud tongue-clicking sound resonates around the cave, and a hand reaches out to help me. I grab it without thinking.

"Hurry up, will you?" Cole whispers.

His husky, hushed voice twists up my stomach, ripples like water across my cheeks, and trickles between my breasts.

I almost let go, but Trent's whistle echoes around the stone from below. "Here, kitty, kitty, kitty."

Cole presses me against the back of the alcove, covering my body with his.

Rivulets of sweat drip down my neck, and I open my mouth to speak, but he covers it with his palm. He shakes his head. The darkness around us is thick and unnatural. Magic tickles my skin as he extinguishes the pixie dust glow with an unknown spell. The cold trickle of water around my calves stops, the spell apparently drying my clothes too.

"I know you're close, mortal. I can smell the fear rolling off you," Trent says.

Cole closes his eyes, his lips move silently, and his body creeps closer. A thin, long-sleeved black shirt hugs his muscular body and scrapes the red wool of my jacket. The brush of fabric makes my head spin, his unearthly magic so intoxicating that I'm drunk with it.

If he was to bend down and replace his hand with his mouth, I'd spontaneously combust. I imagine him kissing me, and my lids flutter. The Fae thrall punches me in the throat, and I fall flat on my metaphorical witch ass.

A high-pitched scream bursts through the cavern. I wonder for a second if it's coming from me, but no. Trent grunts and runs out.

Cole gives me an inch of space and lets his arms fall to his sides.

I'm still reeling from the first brush of his fingers on mine. The imprint of his silky skin tingles across my palm. I massage the calluses to get rid of the sparks buzzing across my nerves, but it's no use.

Cole's eyes follow my movements. "You should have shaken my hand the other day. Would have gotten that first touch out of the way in a safe space."

"This isn't safe?" I croak.

One corner of his mouth quirks up. "Not as safe as a classroom full of people."

The dude not only looks like a block of marble, but he feels like one. His body pins me in place, and I hold up my hands to push him away but only manage to flatten my palms on his upper chest.

A gruff, masculine chuckle falls off his lips. "If you wanted to cop a feel, all you had to do was ask."

I jerk my hands off him. "Why did you help me?"

"If he caught you up here, he would have seen me. I have no desire to waste my time doing chores all month."

"But you lured me here." I say the words without thinking and wonder where they came from. What the hell?

The arch of Cole's brow is asking the same question. "I don't know what you're talking about, Sabrina. You found me all on your own." He leans against the wall at his back, giving me an inch of space to breathe. "Now, let's just wait here for another ten minutes."

I bite the insides of my cheeks until I draw blood and count the seconds in my head. 1. 2. 3. 4—

"I'm going to have to find a new hideout," Cole says.

"Been using this a lot, have you?"

"It's useless now. We'll both be seekers next time, and unless we both squeeze in here every time we have to hide, I know you're going to rat me out as soon as you're found."

The prospect of being *squeezed* by the cocky Fae prince on a bi-monthly basis doesn't sound as alarming as it should to my delirious, adrenaline-filled ears. "I won't be found next time. Won't have that damn pixie dust all over me. And I couldn't care less if you are found or not."

"Playing it tough, I see."

"You're the only player here."

He chuckles again, but this time it's an honest sound. The least sarcastic sound that's come out of him since we met. "You're funny, Sabrina."

"Jules."

"I know."

"Then use it," I clip. Fire rises to the surface of my skin and licks my ribs, shoulders, and arms.

Cole watches the sudden, magical glow with interest. "Not so hot, Fire Girl. You'll lead them right to us." He picks a small piece of lint off my jacket.

Fire Girl. It's better than Sabrina, and a grin tugs at the corners of my mouth.

"I see you, Cole. What are you doing with that witch?" Flynn's melodic but hollow voice slices through the air.

Cole's jaw twitches, and he throws his friend a dispassionate look over the edge of our hideout.

"We're at number 19. Be a man about it and do what needs to be done," Flynn says. An unspoken menace simmers at the edges of his congenial tone. "Or is something else going on up there?"

Cole grazes my hair with his knuckles. "Sorry, Sabrina. Like you said earlier, it's every man for himself." He shoves me out of the alcove, and I plummet 20 feet down to the bottom of the cave. The moss barely absorbs the impact, and the whiplash knocks the wind out of me.

Flynn grins ear-to-ear and pokes my forehead. "Lucky number 20." He turns to his friend. "You can come out, now."

Blood runs down my fingers when I pat down my injured head.

Cole falls to his feet with the grace and aloofness of a house cat and dusts off his pants. "Tough break." He offers me his hand.

I glower, still too dizzy to move but too proud to show it. "I don't need your help."

Cole raises a brow. "Then why are you still lying on the ground?"

I shuffle to my ass and wipe a dark wave away from my face. "You won. Just leave."

"Whoops. You mortals are squishier than Fae fruit." Flynn collects a bit of blood from the back of my head. "Should have kept that helmet on." His leer slides down my body. "I wonder if you taste as sweet as you smell."

Mortified, I realize my skirt is hiked up to my hips, my black cotton panties on display. My mind and limbs turn to stone as Flynn descends upon me.

I yank the plaid down, pawing at it like I'm covering up my dirtiest secret.

Flynn's dark light eclipses Cole completely. His proximity makes everything else around him fade to black. I try to move, but my legs have more in common with overcooked spaghetti than they do with functioning muscles.

"The game is over, pet. But we could still have fun. What do you say?"

I swallow against the roil in my stomach. "I've had quite enough fun for one night."

Cole stretches his arms over his head. "She's not interested, mate." The boredom on his face is both obvious and hateful in the face of my predicament.

Flynn huffs. "Who is she kidding? She'd beg for it within a minute."

The blond Fae's predatory gaze picks at a loose thread inside me until my righteous anger unspools into a tangle of ice. The whiplash of the head injury dulls my powers, and I suddenly realize I'm alone with two tall, heavily muscled men. Two incredibly powerful Fae could easily manipulate me into submission.

"Do you want a kiss, darling?" The deep tone slithers inside my cells, Flynn's beautiful face a mere inch from mine.

Some part of my brain knows what's happening, but my lips are warm and hungry. It doesn't feel like the mind control spells I read about. I can move or spit in his face, but I don't want to. I want to be crushed by those full lips and discover the taste of them on my tongue. I crave nothing but his touch.

Flynn Verinos brushes my cheek with his thumb, and I want to submit to him. To know what it feels like to be broken apart and put back together by his expert kiss. I know nothing in this realm might ever compare...

If he kisses me, maybe some of that light inside his skin, that delicious immortality, will seep into me.

It is magic at its most primitive state. Temptation. Seduction. His powers smother me from all sides. They cut off my oxygen and sanity until I'm panting.

At the last possible second, Cole grabs Flynn by the shoulders and pulls him toward the entrance of the cave. "Come on, let's not waste our time on an ugly mortal."

Something passes between them. Flynn's face shrinks. Cole glowers.

Fists curl against thighs. Cole's jaw ticks.

Finally, the tension in Flynn's back eases. "You're right. I bet she's a cold fish anyway."

Their silhouettes disappear around the corner, and I let go of the breath I'd been holding, but the air catches in my throat. Tears wet my cheeks, and I swipe them away with the back of my wrinkled white blouse.

Ugly mortal.

I'm not sure which word sounded foulest rolling off Cole's tongue, which cruel inflection of his smooth, husky voice cut into me the deepest. Hate simmers inside me as I sit here, bloodied and humiliated. Some part of my brain is still caught in the dark fascination and restless energy I felt when we were alone. Flynn's magic shattered me. Some debased, primeval part of me was prepared to kneel at their feet and service their needs.

Acid rises in my mouth and chases away the taste of blood and tears. I can handle punches and scrapes. What I can't handle is being robbed of my self-worth by some dark Fae mojo.

There's got to be an antidote. Some sort of spell to ward myself against these beasts.

Cole Desyris is not worth my tears or smiles, not worth a puff of my breath. He's only worth the salt needed to resist him.

9

RAISE YOUR GLASS

*T*hey corral the losers into a meadow near the main path. I'm both sad and relieved to see Lydia among them.

A big five is tattooed across her neck. "Hey. Who got you? Melanie found me in two seconds."

"Flynn got me," I say.

Lydia squeezes my arm. "Are you okay? You're awfully pale. Shit— You're bleeding. Did Flynn hurt you?"

"Not really. I bumped my head." I fluff my hair to hide the wound.

"Did he steal your helmet? Because there are policies in the student handbook against bullying."

A dry laugh pops out of my throat. "I'm sure Flynn would love for me to report him so he can change my nickname from ugly mortal to dirty snitch."

"I guess you're right." She glances around the crowd. "Hey, isn't that your sister?"

My pulse spikes when I finally spot Allie. She's out front celebrating amongst the best hiders, and the spit dries from my mouth.

She didn't warn me. She just let me wander the woods and get caught without an ounce of hesitation. I should have heard about this

Academy tradition from her. Family trumps secret initiations in my book, but nooooooo.

I don't care how many exams she has or how many naps she needs, she's acting like a jerk. It's Middle School all over again. Allie snubbed me for 6 months when she dated her first boyfriend—a bully with a small dick and an even smaller mind—so I shouldn't be surprised, but I thought we were older and wiser now.

The newbies, whether they were found or not, are all forced into a clump where we get stinky mudberries thrown at us. The football-sized fruits stain our skin and clothes with a dirty gray color.

Flynn and Cole are nowhere to be seen. I kick myself inwardly for looking for them in the first place. Still, I'm surprised they didn't come to relish my humiliation.

A bucket of icy water suddenly hits me square in the face, and I spit a mouthful to the ground.

Finally, after a few minutes, Trent waves his arms to get our attention. "Raise your glass with me."

Pixies bristle above our heads and pass around shots of a glowing, orange liquid. My fingers clench around the small glass.

"May we never study through a party. May we always have enough booze to get drunk. May we laugh, fight, and fuck 'till we're too tired to move. In a few years—months for the unlucky bastards in the back—" Trent raises his glass to the handful of students who will graduate this quarter, "we'll be forced to grow up. So let's be kids for tonight!"

The crowd cheers, and we down our glasses in one gulp.

Lydia pours hers onto the ground.

Loud music booms from a small square device on the pedestal Melanie used to give her speech. The ground starts to vibrate with the hot, savage rhythm of the Devilish Angels' new single. The rock band has been at the top of the charts for months.

Mud rolls off my jacket, so I peel it off my arms carefully and wipe my mouth with my undershirt.

A sea of undulating bodies moves to the music on each side of me while I elbow my way to the front.

"What the hell, *sis*? Where were you?" I bark, the resentment in my voice so deep that I'm surprised she hasn't drowned in it yet.

She half-chokes on her wine. "Jules. Hi. Sorry about that." She grazes the number twenty written across my forehead with her thumb.

"Answer the question."

Her casual shrug feels like a knife sinking between my shoulder blades. "I got here late and didn't see you."

"I was covered in pixie dust!" My eyes narrow. Didn't see me? I brace my hands on my hips and use the two and a quarter inches I have on her to stare her down. "Where were you, really? Because you weren't in that forest."

She huffs. "If I wasn't in the forest, I'd have one of those, too." She motions at the stupid number again. "I have a good hiding spot. I'll show you next time."

I press my lips together. She's lying. It's a well-crafted lie, but Allie's my sister.

The fake confidence in her speech doesn't fool me.

My throat is painful and tight.

Why is she lying?

Why doesn't she give a damn about me anymore?

Allie sips on her wine greedily. "Who did you get paired up with in S&S?"

I clamp my mouth shut. If she's not going to talk, then I won't either.

"Who did you get?"

I angle myself away from her and watch the others dance. "A Fae."

She brings her cup to her lips, her knuckles turning white. "Which one?"

"The dark one." I'm being totally childish, pretending that I don't know his name.

She snatches my wrist, and her nails sink into my skin until they draw blood. "You got Cole as your Spell and Sorcery partner?"

There's something unsettling about how she says his name, like she has said it many, many times before. Like her tongue is familiar with the crisp K-sound and luxuriates in the sweet inflection of the "ole."

Her arm shakes, her face green and clammy. Then, like nothing happened, she tucks her hair behind her ear. "He probably won't help you much and let you do all the work. Don't take it personal."

"Allie…"

"I'll see you later."

"Allie!"

I shout at her back, but she breezes toward the main hall as though she's deaf or completely uninterested in continuing this conversation.

The half moon grooves in my skin are red and painful, and I massage my bruised wrist.

Whatever is happening to Allie, Cole is involved, somehow. Gods… Did she sleep with him? The notion is revolting, and bile rises to my mouth.

They might fuck you, if you beg.

Never make a deal with a Fae. You'll end up on your knees…

10

SHADOW

The Academy is worlds away from my old human high school, but it's got a few similarities. Teachers, desks, uncomfortable chairs...And that class you have to take, even though you'd rather push your eyeballs inside out.

A mousy, bald leprechaun with a high voice and a bright green satin suit walks into the room. He's barely three-feet tall, and while we're taught not to judge species by their height, this particular teacher clearly doesn't know how to command a room. He nervously tugs on his slim mustache and waits for us to settle down. "Hello, students. I'm Mr. Wright."

Whispers whistle in the three rows behind me. There are five boys and four other girls. At least, they won't be accused of sexism.

Allie leans in. "He's the Foreign Currencies and Supernatural Trade teacher."

Those two subjects aren't part of the mandatory curriculum, but I know Allie has an interest in accounting. "Are you going to take those?"

"I'd rather choke on a pot of gold," she whispers.

I smile despite the bad joke. Allie is finally acknowledging my existence. That's a step in the right direction.

Mr. Wright becomes redder and redder and finally clears his throat. "Welcome to the special mortal monthly seminar. This is a safe space to discuss the do's and don'ts of a safe mortal environment."

Olson raises his hand. "Do we have to?"

Stifled snickers resonate across the classroom.

"Yes, Mr. Lewis. It's a mandatory credit for mortals."

Leaflets fly to our desks.

The dos and don'ts of mortality. A guide to a safe supernatural education by Edgard C. Wright.

Do get your mandatory stamp at the administration office.

Do educate yourself about immortals.

Do get your food and drinks directly from the cafeteria.

Do wear protective enchantments when possible.

Do be respectful of the immortal's customs, even if they appear shocking to you.

Err—Condescending much?

Don't go out alone at night.

Don't fraternize with predatory species.

Don't consume dubious foods or liquids.

Don't tease or provoke immortals in any way.

Don't wear bright colors or show too much skin.

That last one turns the sarcasm simmering in my mouth to pure venom. "This is abuser mentality!"

Mr. Wright jumps at my outburst. "We want you to survive." The leprechaun's thick thighs strain against his green pants as he walks over to me. We're at eye-level since I'm sitting, and he sizes me up like I'm nothing but a rock stuck in his shoe. "There's all types of species here, Miss Winslow. Wearing a skirt like that will attract unwanted attention."

Jaw clenched, I instinctively tug on the end of my skirt. "It's a uniform, dumbass," I murmur under my breath. My knuckles turn white, and I force my fist back open, unwilling to further legitimize his lewd comment. "Why shouldn't the immortals have a seminar on how not to be homicidal jackasses?"

I get a few laughs and claps at that, and a sense of pride and vindication swells in my chest. We didn't choose the uniforms, and we certainly didn't choose this class.

The teacher glowers. "Immortals are not used to your weak constitutions."

I bounce to my feet. "Immortals are condescending jerks!"

"Miss Winslow, you leave me no choice but to emit a final warning. Sit and read the material provided, or I'll refer you to the Headmistress' office." His voice quiets down in a vile, insidious whisper.

I'm about to tell him where he can put his dumb leaflet when Allie grasps my lower arm.

Her eyes are wide, and her shaky fingers skim my wrist. "Sit down, Jules."

Mr. Wright tucks his double chin up. "Listen to your sister, Miss Winslow. She knows how things work here."

I bite my tongue but slump to my ass next to Allie.

"What the hell?" I mouth silently.

She shakes her head and turns her attention to the leaflet.

I grumble, but follow suit. "I guess it's better than human math."

With a wistful look on her face, she stares off into space. "High school wasn't so bad."

"You're telling me you miss physics?" I say mockingly.

"Sometimes." She shrugs again. As much as she's been abusing the gesture, her shoulders should hurt from the effort.

Mr. Wright clicks his purple tongue. "You can gossip on your own time, Miss Winslow."

I force my attention back to the offending document and glare intently at it until the seminar is over. By "safe space to discuss mortal issues," the leprechaun clearly meant "read silently and leave me the fuck alone." My face is still heated, my blood boiling with all the witty comebacks I should have thrown at him, starting with how his name was ill-chosen, considering he's wrong about everything he intends to teach us about ourselves.

GARGOYLES GUARD the entry to the huge Dark Falls library. They lounge along the rails of the staircase leading to the entrance. The tallest one has a large forehead, protruding bottom jaw, and viciously pointy teeth. It yawns loudly as I draw near. Its large wings crack, and the rigid arch of its back set my teeth on edge.

The impenetrable eyes of the moving statue swirl to life. "Name?"

"Julia Winslow."

It nods, fluffs its leathery wings, and settles back into its slumber. Hugging my bag to my chest, I thud up the steps.

Thunder rumbles through the sky.

The entrance to the building is majestic. There are two round staircases on each side, and a monumental chandelier hangs in midair above my head. The tiny flames of the golden candlesticks shimmer and give the austere atmosphere a bit of warmth. I read in the Dark Falls brochure that it's the only one of its kind in the world. It burns continuously without dropping a hint of wax, and it's unaffected by the wind.

The book stacks are on the second and third floor and wrap around the walls from all sides, towering above the study hall.

A series of leather bound volumes are set out front, and I flip through one quietly. It's a reference system that works with magic.

I bite my bottom lip, unsure. It's only the second day so I have no assignments, yet.

The volume opens to a page, and the title "The Witches of Dark Falls" appears, flanked by a few dark alphabet letters. I scribble them on a slip and climb up the stairs. Once again taken by the grandeur of it all, I clench the banister, and my mouth dries up at the mountains and mountains of rare books within my reach.

The other students shuffle in, so I tuck the piece of paper in my blazer's pocket, stowing it for later and sprawl out on the table farthest away from the teacher's desk. Rain starts hammering on the floor-to-ceiling windows, each *tap tap tap* louder than the last.

A man walks to the front, sits on the reference desk, and raps his fingers against his dark blue jeans. "Hello, class. For those of you newbies, I'm Daniel Osbourne, Duel coach and Guided Studies teacher extraordinaire."

I arch a brow at his green wool polo, and my ears perk up. My first Duel class is tomorrow. I'm positively vibrating with nerves at the prospect. At least the teacher looks cool.

A warm smile tops his masculine face.

The pixie twins sit right in front of him and bat their eyelashes dreamily.

Cole stalks off to the back table in the opposite corner. His court is nowhere to be seen, and the twins are too busy drooling over Mr. Osbourne to hover around him.

He unpacks his leather bag. A pen is tucked behind his pointy ear, and his gaze wanders in my direction.

I school my sight back on the teacher and wait a few seconds before I steal another glance.

A mischievous smile plays with the corners of his mouth like he's privy to some big secret.

I clutch my pencil and angle my chair away from him.

I need to concentrate on Mr. Osbourne's instructions.

The seasoned students are to study quietly. The newbies have to familiarize themselves with the reference system, each of us is assigned a list of ten books to locate in the mayhem upstairs.

After climbing the stairs to the third floor, I rest a tall ladder on a particularly skewed stack and check that it's steady. I'd never admit to a fear of heights, but I sure hope that the next book on my list will not be so far up. I climb, search for the right edition, and finally close my hand around the desired spine.

A dark shadow slithers from the front panel and wraps its black tail around my wrist. I hold my breath as it probes my arm. Black little lines form on my skin. Ink flashes in and out of view like a thousand little runes are hiding beneath the dermis and stretching to life. What the actual fuck?

Books are alive. Every supernatural knows that, but they usually don't attack people.

A cold patch spreads along the shadow's trajectory and gives my skin a purple tint.

I yank my hand off the shelf and clench the ladder.

The shadow gives chase. I zap it with a burst of heat. With a loud whoosh, the book in my hand catches on fire. Flames burst out of the pages, and the shadow hisses before jumping into my hand. Spooked, I jerk back and feel my foot slip from the ladder.

Pain burns across my palm as I fall, and my body hits the floor with a crack.

I can't breathe.

The whole class erupts in laughter.

The librarian, an old woman with lizard print glasses and a nose pointy enough to pierce skin, flies in my direction. "Vandalizing school property, Miss Winslow?"

I graze the nasty burn on my wrist and wince. "There was something up there."

Her small, translucent wings twitch rapidly. "And what was that? A goblin? A ghost?"

"A shadow." My lids flutter shut at how squeaky my voice sounds.

"I forget how jumpy you mortals are. Well, it's too late now. This is ruined." She sighs at the burnt book like she would rather have seen me go up in flames than it. Her purple gaze falls on something behind me. "Mr. Desyris. Take her to the infirmary."

My jaw slacks. Cole is standing a mere foot away. Two leather-bound books are propped under his arm.

He blinks once. Twice. "Why me?"

"Because I'm telling you." Without a second glance, the librarian whizzes back to the tray of volumes waiting to be sorted.

Cole grunts and spins around, heading out of the library. I follow, my heart still doing championship acrobatics in my chest. What happened up there? Where did this shadow come from?

The Fae prince slows down once we're outside. Puddles splash against my soles, but the rain has stopped.

He snatches my injured wrist and holds it to the light. "So peculiar.

A fire witch not immune to fire." Melodic bells seems to echo in his inhuman voice.

The sound softens my legs. "Fire didn't do this."

"It was a shadow?" he says mockingly.

I dig the balls of my feet in the ground. "I can find my way from here."

He arches a brow. "Are you dismissing me?"

"Yes." There. That ought to be clear enough for him.

"Oh, come on. I want to know all about the evil that haunts our beloved library."

I stomp off, but he's quick on my heels.

"You're still here?" I growl.

"Mr. Oz will ask if you got to the infirmary in one piece."

"Say that I did."

"It'd be a lie."

I snort. "Like you never lie."

He wets his lips. "What do you figure I lie about?"

"Everything." I try to keep my answers short and dismissive, and yet he's still following. We're almost to the cafeteria.

"You'd be right." A confident chuckle strikes me in place. The sound goes straight to my belly and sends a burst of heat to my neck. "But I do make an exception for when I'm escorting mortals to the infirmary," he adds mysteriously.

I swallow hard. "Got a lot of experience, eh?"

"Some." The rogue curve of Cole's mouth perplexes me with its warmth.

As we near the building, the closest door leading to the cafeteria swings on its hinges.

Jessa, the Fae girl with blue hair and those impossible cheekbones, struts in our direction. She stops abruptly when she spots us. "What's going on?"

Cole's casual swag immediately stiffens, and I swear he skirts around me so that we're farther apart. "Nothing."

"You walking within four feet of *that* is not nothing."

I should really walk past her and ignore the jab, but I can't. Instead,

I stop an inch from her face and glare into her damn beautiful blue eyes. The color is so rich it's dizzying. "I've got a name."

The hint of boredom lifts from her face, which becomes alive with vicious happiness. "It speaks."

Cole wraps an arm around her and pulls her to him. "She fell in the library. Old Pembrooke had me escort her to the infirmary."

Jessa twists in his arms, her raptor gaze fixed on me. "That old bird really hates you. You shouldn't have defied the sanctity of the written words."

"If I remember correctly, I wasn't the one sprawled on the priceless copy of A Gargoyle's Life," Cole jokes, the inflection of his voice so intimate that I blush.

Jessa leans in for a kiss.

Somehow, I've missed my cue to leave and end up staring at them as they make out. It's ten times worse than with Flynn and Mel, and while I know I have to screw my eyes shut and walk away, I'm glued to my spot, dying inside from my total inability to stop this train wreck.

"We have a peeping Sally." Jessa spins to face me. "Are you into him?" She plays with Cole's collar, and her glossy lips quirk. "Or into me?" She clicks her tongue. "Or maybe you're just another Winslow whore."

The haze shatters into a million pointy glass shards. "Don't talk crap about my sister."

"I was referring to your two-timing Dad, but sure, your sister fits the bill, too."

I push her. I physically push her with all my might.

She almost stumbles to the ground, but Cole catches her in time and pulls her back to her feet. Jessa's mouth opens in clear outrage, but Cole's tight expression is unreadable.

My hands crackle with fire magic.

Jessa's blue eyes narrow down to slits. "What's your trauma, freak?"

I don't know. Sure, what she said was not okay, but physical violence is strictly prohibited. Attacking a Fae in broad daylight is probably the stupidest thing I've ever done.

A few students stare wide-eyed from the windows. Shit. Shit. Shit. I could get in real trouble for this.

Before I accidentally throw a fireball at Jessa, I bury my hands in my pockets, tuck my shoulders in, and barrel into the cafeteria. Taking the stairs two at a time, I'm halfway to the infirmary when a hauntingly beautiful voice resonates around the staircase.

"Run, run, little mouse. The cat's hungry for you now," Brie chants in my wake. The cruel edge of her siren voice cracks my soul.

I crane my neck around and catch her smirking up at me. Her short green hair flows around her head like we're underwater, and my chest constricts.

Looks like I won't be safe in the ocean anytime soon.

11

FIRE GIRL

"*P*arty at the falls tonight, my pretties." Melanie sits between Lydia and I at the dining table and slaps both our thighs. Her leather and chains outfit is wrapped tightly around her curvy figure, and a black choker ensnares her white throat. A few clip-on hair extensions lengthen her mane to her waist, and her eyeliner resembles a spiderweb at the corners of her eyes.

I push around the cold carrot left on my plate. "I'm good."

Mel pouts. "Oh, come on. First week of quarter is made for parties."

"We still have a ton of chores to do," Lydia says.

We've been put on dishes duty for the rest of the month.

Mel waves dismissively. "Hurry up and join us after. The Falls party is iconic. Everyone comes."

"I'm tired," I grumble. A party will just be a new opportunity for disaster, and I've met my quota this week.

Mischief shines in the vampire's ruby eyes. "Right. I heard you freaked out in Guided Studies and fell down. I guess it's normal for mortals to be tired." The taunt in her voice is crystal clear. Don't be a baby and prove to everyone that you're as tough as us, or go to bed and validate the gossip.

I press my tongue to the roof of my mouth. "Fine. We'll go."

"Yay! See you there." She ruffles my hair and struts away, her hips swinging to imaginary music.

You've got to give it to the girl. She really marches to the beat of her own Goth drums. She meets up with her twin, Trent, near the entrance, links her arm in his and pulls him along.

Lydia and I finish up the dishes around 10:00 pm. My fingers are cramped from the relentless waving and snapping. The rebellious enchanted brushes fought us at every turn, unwilling to stop galli-vanting around the kitchen and do their damn jobs. It's still eons faster than the human way, and we're not covered in dirty water, but the task is utterly frustrating.

"I think I'm heading to bed. I've got my first Creatures From Other Realms class tomorrow at five," Lydia says on a yawn.

"I've got Duel." I look down at my black t-shirt and wrinkled uniform skirt. It's not fit for a party.

"You should get a good night sleep. I heard that class is brutal."

"I've got to make an appearance." I let my hair loose and ruffle it to give it some volume, and roll the hem of the plaid until it's above my mid-thigh. Better.

Lydia hands me her red lipstick. "Fuck 'em. You fell, it's no big deal."

I apply a thin coat to my lips with the brush. It's glossy but thick, and the color really pops. After checking my reflection in the cafeteria mirror, I smack my lips together, satisfied with the result, and give the glossy tube back. "Actually, there really was a shadow."

Her eyes narrow. "What did it look like?"

I explain everything in detail. The flare of dark energy, the cold patch, the purple skin.

She shakes her head. "Sounds like you were hit by a curse."

"A curse?" My brows raise. I didn't even think of that.

Curses are an old form of magic. It takes a very skilled Magus to weave one, and even then they are volatile as fuck. If someone tried to curse me...

"It's probably nothing," I say. "I'll tell you if you missed anything."

"Like what? Blane eating his shoe?" my roommate jokes.

"Exactly." I grab a napkin and remove the excess lipstick from my lips.

"It's a no-smudge batch. My mother enchanted it," Lydia says casually.

"That's so cool." I examine my reflection with new interest and glide my thumb against my bottom lip, but sure enough, the colorful lipstick stays where it belongs. Dad never taught us to do that. I guess he never knew how useful that would be.

It's not the first time I'm reminded, even in the smallest way, that I didn't have a mother to teach me those things, but tonight, it stings more.

A heavy lump settles in my throat. "Good night."

"Night." Lydia leaves, oblivious to my dark mood.

I start the hike to the elusive Dark Falls, the beautiful waterfalls after which the Academy was named. The path is sprinkled in moonlight, and I walk deeper and deeper into the unending woods. Between Allie's behavior and the way mortals are patronized, this new life isn't quite as wonderful as I wished it to be.

With Dad, we traveled all the time, switching houses almost every year to follow his Ministry career around wherever he was needed. I'd figured spending three to four years in one place would be heaven, but now...

The leafless, skeletal trees encroach onto the path, and the trail in front of me becomes narrower with every step. The light dims as a big cloud glides in front of the moon. Vicious caws resonate across the trunks. My heartbeat spikes, but I curl my hands into fists and continue up the mountain.

I won't let them be right about mortals. I won't wash out or let the staff bully me into acting like a scared little girl.

I'm a Winslow witch, and we don't take crap from anyone. We don't back down.

A loud branch cracks, and two golden eyes stare at me from the shadows.

"Who's there?"

The eyes disappear, but a low growl simmers in the dark.

I snatch a thick branch from the ground, hold it up, and close my eyes. Powers crackles from the tips of my fingers, and the dry wood catches on fire. The makeshift torch reveals a second path heading deeper into the forest, large animal footsteps etched into the mud. All the hairs on my body rise to attention. My breath quickens.

A large shadow looms over me, its tendrils held away by the fire. It's as big as a house but translucent, and I gape at it, blinking wildly.

"What are you?" I ask.

It hisses and extinguishes my fire with one dry cry before it plunges to my feet. Despite my earlier promises for bravery, I run. My legs scream from the crazy pace as the shadow chases me uphill.

Its gnarled claws lick my heels.

Music booms above the rustling of the branches and the heavy beats of my heart. A green light pierces the darkness. My pulse staggers when a bonfire comes into view. Loud laughter erases the chill in my bones.

I spin around, but there's nothing behind me, and I force my breathing back to normal. If I burst into a party claiming a shadow lurks in the forest, it'd be social suicide.

Leaves crack under my soles.

A thirty foot fall spills loudly into a round, glassy lake in three separate streams. Water tumbles and roars downward. Green, red, yellow, and blue party lights transform it into a hypnotic rainbow. A few students I don't recognize are lounging on the big rocks flanking the water.

I tuck my hair behind my ears and straighten my shirt. The bonfire dances in the breeze. A sea of bodies drink and sway around it, all of them having more fun than me. The stink of cheap alcohol and musk pervades the air.

Maybe it's the adrenaline, but all the happy faces blur together, and I bump into a table full of empty plastic cups and stop to search for Melanie, Allie, or any other friendly face.

"Fire Girl. You came." Cole greets me. He skips right into my bubble.

I roll my shoulders back and inch backward. I feel vulnerable and lightheaded, so I can't handle his glamor right now.

The top three buttons of his crisp, black button-down shirt are open, his tie nowhere to be found. His glassy amber eyes are swimming in booze, and his sleeves are rolled to his elbows, showing off his forearms. The tall, marble-like stature once again steals my tongue.

He aligns his cup underneath the Pixie Ale brew keg and pushes the button. Beer pours from the tap. "You look pale as a ghost. Did a shadow chase you here?" A light smile plays with the corners of his mouth.

My eyes narrow, and for the first time, I consider him a suspect. Could he have done it? Made this spectral form attack me? To what end? Scare me? Humiliate me?

"Come and play Truth, Dare, or Spell with us," he slurs. The offer sounds more like a command, and I half-expect him to snatch my wrist and pull me along.

There's a peculiar pause, like he catches himself short of doing that exact thing. His hand hangs awkwardly in mid-air. The smooth muscles of his shoulders ripple underneath his shirt.

"No. I'm good." I walk straight past him and ignore the hard curve of his mouth.

I make it three steps beyond the fire before Melanie wraps her arm around me.

"Newbies go skinny dipping the first night," she says.

"I prefer not to drink and swim."

Melanie pouts again. "Alcohol doesn't work as fast on me. I need a distraction."

"Sucks for you." I raise my glass with a big, ear-to-ear grin and gulp down half. The acrid taste of beer calms my nerves.

Loud giggles erupt from the back, and I steal a glance at the crowd.

One of the pixie twins is sitting on Cole's chest, pinning him to the grass, while the other kisses him upside down. His eyes are covered with a silk scarf while they explore his chest with their Barbie fingers.

Everyone in the circle laughs and cheers.

Disgusting.

I whip around and spot Allie standing next to the bonfire. The firelight dances on her face, and her pastel make-up glistens. She's crying.

What the— I half-jump over a large rock and hurry to her side. "What's going on?"

"Nothing." She furiously wipes her cheeks and leaves like being seen with me is the ultimate humiliation. She heads over to the Truth, Dare, or Spell crowd.

I take another swig of beer and slump down on the rock I just passed to observe the dancers. They all look so carefree and chipper. Why can't I be like them?

Three roundtrips to the kegs heighten my buzz, but the ache in my chest only worsens.

Lydia was right. I shouldn't have come.

Melanie climbs on behind me, her tall leather boots creaking on the stone. "Why so glum, witch?"

"Allie hates me now," I grumble.

She dangles her legs from the edge. "Your sister is a snob—no offense. Come on girl, let's dance." She twines our fingers and pulls me into the fray.

I'm wobbly, but I manage not to fall to my ass.

The alcohol lowered my inhibitions, and I find that Melanie is the perfect dance partner. Fun, energetic, and crazy enough to divert attention from me. Her moves attract a bunch of whistles, and she grins happily, her blouse tied in a knot right below her breasts.

When she pries my own black uniform tee from my skirt and ties it in the same way, revealing my belly-button ring, the whistles intensify. I roll with it and follow my vampire friend into a low hip roll. Hip hop music echoes in my bones. My arms fly in the air.

It's how Allie and I would dance when it was just to two of us.

Trent cuts in and makes me twirl. "You look like you're having fun, Julia."

"Jules," I correct him.

He's not Cole-tall, but he's taller than me. He rests his hand at the small of my back and nods to the corner of the meadow. "You see, these clowns dared me to get you to kiss me. They gave me really good odds because they're convinced that you won't."

He's so different from Melanie. The jeans and white t-shirt make him look almost human. His long hair isn't tied behind his head now and gives him a young, hip look. I usually don't find guys with long hair sexy, but Trent's locks don't look greasy or flat, just disheveled.

I've never kissed a vampire before. Nor any other boy of the non-human quality.

My mouth is dry as I consider his demand. "What if you win the round?"

"They all owe me a favor." Mischief dances in his ruby eyes, the color warmer and not at all as jarring as you'd expect.

There's no heat emanating from his hand, and goosebumps scatter across my back. "Do my chores for the rest of the month, and I'll kiss you."

"That's not...You got dishes, right?"

"Going once."

He pouts in the cutest way possible, his vampire face twisted in surrender. "A week. I'll do them for a week."

"Going twice..."

"Alright, alright. A favor from them is worth more than a few hours of sleep. But it's got to look good. Tongue and everything." His smile turns wolfish, and his gaze slides down the slope of my neck to my pulse point.

"No bite. Just a kiss."

"We'll see." His tone is low and seductive. His hands nestle in the hollow above my hipbones.

A discreet heat tingles up my belly. "Just a kiss."

"As you wish." The hungry look on his face doesn't relent.

I snake my hands around his neck. "Deal."

They're all looking at us. Jessa, Krystel, Melanie, Naomi, Flynn, Allie, Jeremy, and Cole.

I grab a fist of Trent's long wavy hair and crush my mouth to his.

Whistles and claps echo in my ears.

His lips are colder than I expected. They frost an icy path down my spine, but it's not bad. In fact, after the initial shock subsides, it's kind of nice. Fresh.

I crack one eye open to look at our audience.

Cole and Jessa aren't there anymore.

"How about that bite now?" Trent trails off.

"Erm—No..." But the "no" is ambiguous and shaky. I've got half a mind to guide him to a dark corner and let him have his bloodthirsty way with me. A vampire bite, when it's friendly, is described as sensuous and overwhelming, and I'm suddenly very curious.

Damn creatures of the night.

A sudden dizziness prevents me from acting on this new desire, and I use his shoulder to catch myself from falling.

"Are you okay?" he asks.

Without another word, I stagger a few steps away from the fire and vomit in the grass.

CHERRIES AND PEACHES

*T*he duel sandpit is as big as a football field. Two wide sets of bleachers stand on either side of the path leading to the middle of the arena, and tall dunes encircle the oval-shaped training ground. My palms are sweaty, and I discreetly wipe them on my leggings before climbing the left bleachers. Trent sits alone in the middle, his extended arms resting against the beam behind him. The Fae and Brie are sitting on the highest step, and the other students crowd the first few rows. About fifteen students in total, which makes Duel the smallest class yet.

Trent straightens up as I draw near. "Hey, Jules."

"Hi." I scan the faces again, but I'm pretty sure I'm the only mortal. Great.

Trent dusts off the area right next to him. "You nervous?"

"Am I that transparent?" I fold my leg below me. This is the only class where we can wear the school's sportswear instead of the traditional uniforms. The black leggings and Lycra shirt highlight my curves, and a hood covers my hair. I feel like a cat burglar.

Trent's shirt hugs his broad chest when he leans forward and sniffs the air above my shoulder. "I can smell it."

The red elastic of my side braid is nestled between my breasts.

Trent steals a long, obvious glance, and I push him away playfully. "Keep your nose in your corner, Darkwood. And your teeth."

He smiles, and I don't hate how his eyes shine or the flirty undertones of the exchange.

The kiss was fine. No, the kiss was good.

He held my hair while I puked my heart out yesterday. I thought he would shove me in the friend zone, but apparently my barfing habits aren't as deterring as I'd thought.

The back of my neck prickles from the hateful glare of the Fae sitting behind me.

Trent brushes my shoulder. "You made an enemy yesterday."

I hug my knees. A handful of students stroll in and sit in the other section. From the skirts and blazers, I gather they aren't here to partake in the class.

"People can watch us fight?" I ask, surprised.

"Are you kidding? Half the boys here only take the class because they want to get laid."

I wet my lips. "Which half are you?"

He wiggles his brows suggestively, and I smack his arm.

Mr. Osbourne whistles, the sound made thunderous by an amplification spell. His voice resonates across the dunes. "Welcome to Duel class, better known as the get-your-ass-kicked-weekly-by-choice extravaganza."

The students snicker, and a few "you're going down" and "pray for your mama" resonate across the sand.

Mr. Oz looks different here than he did yesterday at the library. He takes up more space. His feet dig into the sand with a large gap between them, and his back is straight. The inquisitive gray eyes stare right at us in turn. "You're either here because you want to show off or because you want to try your hand at one of the most dangerous and selective career paths in the three realms. Make no mistake, half the students from last quarter are gone, and half of you will not return. This is not only about raw power, this is about strategy and cunning. If I didn't fail half of you, I wouldn't be doing my job. It's not shameful, either. Not everybody is made for this life."

The sand scratches underneath his shoes as he strolls closer to the bleachers. "We'll do one-on-one skirmishes for now, so I can see what the newbies are made of. Alphabetical order. The first one to yield has to write an essay on his opponent's powers and why they failed to beat them for next week." He peeks at his notepad. "Bastiani and Desyris. Will you do the honors?"

Cole peels himself off his seat and stretches gingerly, arms above his head. From my lower position on the steps, I catch a glimpse of his bare stomach. With a slightly bored expression, he climbs down, not sparring Trent or me a glance.

An imp with small leathery wings is already in position in the middle of the pit.

Flynn brings his hands on either side of his mouth. "Ladies and gentlemen, I give you your Prince. Today, he'll be flattening bad-hair Marco."

The crowd shouts out encouragements and whistles.

Little red horns stick out of the imp's shaggy brown hair, and my heart goes out to the guy. Nobody is cheering for him, except maybe me. The audience is under Cole's spell. The applause doubles when he takes his place in the circle.

His frosty amber gaze roams the crowd.

Our eyes meet for a fleeting moment, and it's like a million snowflakes are falling down my windpipe, stinging my insides as they melt.

I swallow hard but keep my head high.

I can't show him he's getting in my head even though he is. I can't shake the impression he's putting on a show for my benefit, but that's crazy. He just wants to impress his groupies.

A shiver rattles my ribcage, and a stormy wind blows the hood off my head.

Cole snaps his fingers. All of the sudden, eight copies of himself circle quietly around Marco. They are all wearing his trademark smirk.

Marco glances at each one of them in turn.

I draw a sharp intake of breath. Mirror image is an expert-level spell, and a pretty cool one at that. I'd kill to be able to cast it so seam-lessly. Last time I tried, my reflections were glitch-y and in black-and-white.

The flawless mirror images of Cole extend their hands, and black wisps of energy crackle from his hands.

My mind flashes back to the shadow I saw in the library, and a bitter ball stings my throat.

It doesn't look exactly the same. The Fae's powers give off a bluish, electric current, but it's close.

The Coles in the pit lunge straight for Marco.

The imp braces his hands over his head. "I yield."

Cole towers over his opponent, his nostrils flaring. A disgusted grimace twists his features for a second before a mask of pride and superiority eclipses the darker, moody vibe. The prince returns to his seat.

Trent is next. Blane faces him and transforms into a snake. The scales on his skin stretch and contract until a menacingly long, two-hundred pound snake hisses over the sand.

The vampire looks even paler than usual.

Blane's nasty teeth snap the air. He moves so fast that his head blurs, but Trent ducks in time to avoid the bite. I clap and shout out an encouragement. A few heads turn in my direction.

The vampire's arms are stretched on each side of his body. The mass of scales in front of him slithers, and they slowly dance from right to left and left to right.

My friend manages to pin Blane below him and crushes the snake's neck to the ground. The tail twists and trashes before it wraps around Trent's midriff. The vampire winces, but his hold around Blane's neck only strengthens. A forked tongue tastes the air before Blane changes back into human form.

A laugh bubbles up my throat when Trent does a little victory dance.

The class continues until only Flynn and I are left. The Fae boy shoots me a predatory glance.

Trent gives me a thumbs up, and I descend into the pit.

Mr. Osbourne scribbles something into his notebook and raises his hand to signal us to wait.

Flynn shakes out his muscles. A big, round cherry, the size of a baseball, appears in his hand.

I raise a brow.

"Cole's favorite fruit is cherries," the Fae boy says.

I crack my fingers one by one. "What a random thing to say."

Flynn's eyes narrow into a thin, cruel line. "Is it? It could explain why he pulled your name out of that hat. Why he lured you into his favorite hideout the other night. He can always tell when a cherry is ripe for the picking."

My cheeks heat up, and I grit my teeth. Flynn thinks I'm a virgin. And fuck, he's right, but I can't let that show. I tie my hair up in a messy bun and give the audience and my tormentor a shrug. "I'm more of a coconut."

"Hey, as long as you're juicy on the inside, I'm game." Flynn licks his lips, and his leer lingers on my breasts.

I grimace.

Oz motions for us to proceed.

Flynn throws the fruit in the air and catches it. "Give me your worst, coconut. I can't wait to crack you open." The cherry in his hand morphs into a coconut. In his boastful, relaxed smile, there's a real threat.

That's when I realize I'm screwed.

The hard-shelled fruit flies for my head, followed by another and another, and I pirouette out of the way at the last second, but they are still coming. I throw a fireball in Flynn's general direction, but he appears and disappears out of thin air, stepping in and out of smooth, glossy portals he conjures with a snap of his fingers.

I can't keep track, but I throw him all the fire I've got.

A harsh kick in my lower back sends me flying face-first into the dirt. I whip my head up and roll away but another kick follows. The bastard wants to physically hurt me.

My bottom lip splits at the impact. Blood and sand choke me for a moment, but I wipe my mouth with my sleeve. I crouch and spin back to Flynn. A third kick launches me in the air, and my head screams as it collides with the ground.

"Stop the fight!" Mr. Osbourne shouts.

Flynn's next kick gets stuck in mid-air. He straightens up and curtsies to the crowd. The applause makes my ears and heart numb. I shuffle to my feet, and Flynn towers above me. His tall silhouette stands between me and the sun, his mouth showing two white rows of teeth.

"That's okay, mortal. Nobody here expects you to be good at this." He leans in. "Do everyone a favor and drop out before we see you cry."

I aim to kick his nuts, but I'm dizzy, and he sidesteps out of reach like the oily eel that he is.

Mr. Osbourne comes running. "Are you okay, Julia?"

"It's Jules. And I'm fine. Why did you interrupt the fight? I didn't yield."

Deep lines crease his forehead. "It's school policy that any student with a head injury is to be seen by the doctor as soon as possible."

"Any mortal student," I add with sarcasm.

Mr. Osbourne's eyes soften, and he looks to the ground for a second. "Yes. It's seems unfair, I know. But you did great, Jules. Really. Flynn is one of the best in the ring, and you burnt an eyebrow."

"I did?" I watch Flynn. He's over by his supporters, celebrating his victory. The end of his white-blond eyebrow is slightly singed.

A grin glazes my lips until I see Jessa whispering in her prince's ear. The sardonic smile stuck on Cole's face rips a hole in my wounded pride.

I dust off my butt and wince. My breaths come in uneven gusts, and my bones scream from Flynn's abuse.

Jeremy walks over to us. "I'll take her to the infirmary, Mr. Oz."

"Thank you, Jeremy. That's really helpful," Oz answers.

A beautiful, eerie song rises from the bleachers. "You know what's easier to crack than an egg? Julia Winslow's head," Brie chants with her hypnotic mermaid voice, and the other students join the chorus of "mortals are fragile and squishy, but none of them bleed quite like Julia and Allie."

They are amused by my injury like it's all a big joke. Like we are a big joke, and they expect us to disappear like bunnies shoved back into a magician's hat.

Acid simmers at the back of my throat, and I take note of the laughs, the dry snorts, the humiliating whistles. Everyone with a smile on their stupid immortal mouths better watch out.

I'll show them. I'll show all of them what fire can do to a pretty face. Especially a smooth, marble-like one.

I'll show them how *ugly* I can be.

13

UNDER PRESSURE

"*Y*ou can go back to class. I'm fine," I say to Jeremy.

The wrestler-shaped werewolf trails behind me with both hands shoved in his Duel uniform's pockets, His wolf-sized thighs stretch the black Lycra. "I don't mind."

I pick up the pace, frustrated. Do students get extra credits for escorting mortals to the infirmary or what?

The glass door of the dining hall closes behind us, and we climb upstairs to the infirmary tucked at the end of the corridor. It consists of four beds separated by faded-blue curtains, the doctor's office, a bathroom, and a private room. There must be someone in the private bed right now, because the door is closed.

A pink-clad girl hops to her feet, and her 4-inch heels clack against the linoleum. Those shoes aren't up to code, but I'm learning that uniform indiscretions are mostly tolerated when they involve shoes or jackets. The girl's pale skin and her garnet irises clue me in that she's a vampire, but she's literally the antithesis of Melanie. Her cinder-blond hair is separated in the middle and falls cleanly on each side of her face, and her lipstick spells bubblegum instead of queen of darkness.

"I'm Vivianne." Her voice is high-pitched and melodic. She flips her hair behind her shoulder.

I mask a cringe. Gisèle Darko from senior year was a vicious hair flipper. I've learned to mistrust them all. "I'm Jules."

"I know who you are," she says with a scoff. From her grimace, I can tell she's insulted that I would think otherwise.

Jeremy hovers behind me. "Hello, Viv."

I turn back to face him. "Why did they sing 'none of them bleed like Julia and Allie?' When did Allie bleed?" I ask the werewolf. If I can't get him to leave me be, I'll at least get information.

The werewolf turns green, his fists balled at his side. "I don't know."

Vivianne tilts her head to the side. "Brie meant that your sister Allie lost her virginity."

"What? That's ridiculous." Gossip travels faster here than at my old high school. Who knew adulthood meant dealing with more mean girls and jocks? It's exactly the same except now they're masquerading as young, responsible adults.

Vivianne quiets down. "Brie changed all the sheets in Queen Mab's dorm one weekend. There was blood and semen all over Allie's bed." The vampire's face wrinkles in disgust.

I swallow the roil in my stomach. "That's a lie." The words taste bitter still because I can't back them with any type of certainty. Maybe Allie did lose her virginity here. Why would that be bad? It wouldn't… Except the old Allie, my carefree sister with a big smile and an even bigger heart, would have told me.

My skepticism only spurs Vivianne on. "Uh-huh. I live below Allie, and she has a secret boyfriend. Brie and I heard them giggle last night. We tried to spy on her and see who the mysterious boy was, but he's sneaky. All our spells bounced off her damn attic door."

My mouth twists downward. "You're Brie's roommate?"

"Yep. She's not as mean as she appears," Vivianne says in her high, pep-filled voice.

I chew on my bottom lip, unconvinced.

"What weekend was this?" Jeremy asks, white as Miss Eillis' hair.

Vivianne shrugs. "Right after the Halloween party."

Jeremy meets my gaze, and his eyes flash with a hint of yellow, his fists shaking at his sides. Before I can try to defuse the situation, the closed exam room opens.

The Academy's doctor, Dr. Chen, slips out, and I catch a glimpse of a bloody foot before she shuts the door.

She straightens her white coat. Her long black hair has the typical silver freckles of a chimera. It's tied is a neat bun at the nape of her neck. Her serious, secretive eyes are two different colors—one green, one pink. "You again?"

A deep sigh quakes my chest. "Me. Again."

"What's the issue?" She passes a hand over her tense face. Her right sleeve is tainted with blood.

"Absolutely nothing." My swollen lip speaks for itself. "I'm here because immortals are dumbasses."

"She hit her head," Jeremy says, still hovering.

He's standing too close behind me, and I've got half a mind to swat him away. He acts like a fly that keeps landing on you and won't give you an inch of space.

"Second time in two days, Miss Winslow. Be careful, or I'll have to pull you from Duel class and recommend a special seminar."

I cross my arms. "I'll be penalized because I got hurt?"

"It's policy." She gives me a reproachful, stern glare and takes my vitals silently. "You don't have to stay, Vivianne. Thank you for bringing your friend in. She's stable for now. She got lucky that you found her." The doctor murmurs a spell, and the gash in my head along with the one on my lip tingle with warmth. "You can go too, Julia. Tell Oz that he better stop sending me students, or I'll start a Duel class of my own." With that, she spins on her heels and enters her office.

Vivianne waits for Dr. Chen to close the door before she answers our unspoken question. "I found a mortal in the woods this morning." She leans toward us. Her eyes gleam with excitement like she's about to drop the juiciest piece of gossip.

Dread builds in my chest. "Who?"

"Holly, I think."

My mind flashes to a small, mousy witch sitting behind me and Allie during the mortal seminar. I heard Olson address her as Holly. "What happened?"

"I don't know. She was unconscious. I was running the trails that loop from the falls to the beach and smelled her. There was blood everywhere, and her uniform was in tatters like she'd been attacked by some kind of animal."

The yellow eyes and the growl I heard yesterday come back to mind, and icicles prickle my ribcage from the inside out. "Where, exactly? Was it near the trail that goes down to the dining hall?"

Vivianne arches a brow. "Why?"

I bite my bottom lip, uncertain. If I blab about the yellow eyes and the shadow to this girl, the whole school will know about it before tomorrow. I grab my head dramatically and wince. "Shit. I need something for the pain." I knock on Dr. Chen's door and wave goodbye to Vivianne and Jeremy.

"Come in," the chimera says quietly.

Crisp teal paint brightens the rectangular office. A mahogany desk towers in the middle, and three small black frames decorate the glossy wood surface. A big copper cauldron simmers on a cooktop.

Vials and flasks clutter the table behind Dr. Chen. Her fingers pause over the keyboard of her laptop. "Have you changed your mind about that seminar?"

"No, I—" The wall is covered with diplomas. Dr. Chen attended Harvard medical school as well as the High Healing Institute, the most recognized supernatural healing program. This makes her one of the most elite minds of our time, and yet she's here playing nurse on my cuts and scrapes. My gut tightens. "I think I might have seen something in the woods yesterday."

She purses her lips. "You think you might have seen something?"

I clear my throat and find enough courage to meet her gaze head-on. "I saw yellow eyes, heard a growl, and ran." I don't know why, but I omit the shadow. Whatever it was, it didn't growl, and it didn't have eyes. Or teeth.

She gets a piece of paper and a pen from her desk. "Write everything you saw, when and where, on here. I'll relay the info to security, and they'll follow up if needed."

I write everything down, minus the shadow, and hand it back to her. "Is Holly going to be okay?"

The doctor's hand twitches over the file in front of her. "She's stable for now," she says, repeating the words she gave Vivianne. "I can't discuss the details with you. Please keep what you saw to yourself. If the attacker knows that you saw him, he might come for you next."

My voice raises in alarm. "It wasn't a beast that attacked her?"

The chimera's serious features tense. "Half the students and staff here are beasts, Miss Winslow. Never forget that."

I nod before exiting the office. Vivianne and Jeremy are gone, and I sigh in relief. I can't escape the thought that it might have been me lying on that bed. Or Allie.

Whatever is going on with her, I can't let it get to me. We're family. Without thought, I hurry out of the infirmary and head for my sister's dorm.

Allie is studying in the backyard behind the Queen Mab building. A few rocks are sprawled out in the late autumn sun, and Allie is perched on the biggest. A book lies across her thighs. One black flat raps the stone below her in a regular motion while her other leg is folded beneath her.

The heaviness in my shoulders recedes. "Hey, you."

Her eyes flick from the page. "Jules, hi. Didn't you have class?"

I point to my mouth. "Cut my lip."

"Their stance on blood is utter bullshit." She reclines on the rock, elbows propped behind her, and angles her face to the sun.

I watch her carefully. Gone are the dark circles and nervous behavior. With her blond locks flying across her cheeks and her pink eye-shadow, she looks just like my Allie. "You look good."

"I am. I'm done with Mastery of Air. I can finally breathe."

"I lost you at the party last night."

A hint of a smile plays at the corners of her lips. "I left early."

"Vivianne says you have a boyfriend…" I trail off. Not the stealthiest approach, but I need to gather clues before she blows me off again. Besides, the mood seems right.

A blush creeps up on her cheeks, and her eyes twinkle with something I've seen in school or movies, but never, ever on my sister's face. "Yes." She tilts her head forward. "Look, I'm sorry I kept it from you, but it's going really well, and I don't want to mess it up. We want things to stay private for a while."

We? If she's saying we, it means it's serious. Allie has never been a we person. I can read it in her shy, giddy smile. She's in love.

I'm torn on how I feel about it. Love is supposed to be a good thing. Secrets and weird behavior, not so much. Love plus secrets and weird behavior equals…trouble? "Who is he?"

She makes a zipping motion over her lips.

"You won't even give me a clue?"

"No. I'll tell you soon, though." She ruffles my hair, and it feels like us again.

I hug my leather bag to my knees. "Can you at least tell me if I know him?"

Mischief dances in her blue eyes. "You do. Of course, you do. We're stuck with each other here."

An itch spreads from my ribs to my neck. "Then tell me."

The elation on her face dims. "Why do you want to know?"

"Why won't you tell me?" From what Vivianne told me, she's having sex with this guy. Shouldn't I know who he is?

She gives me that annoyed older sister look. The one I can't stand because it makes me feel like an immature brat. "I think he wants to get to know you without all the added pressure. He's afraid you're not going to give him a chance."

The itch turns into a blazing heat, and my blood pumps at my temples. "Err—What?"

"Relax, Jules. You'll like him. Promise." With an enigmatic chuckle, she scampers off to class.

A cloud of questions and a sense of impending doom tighten my ribcage.

Allie promised not to break my Barbie once...Dad scraped off melted plastic from his barbecue for months.

I'm supposed to walk around campus and wonder which of the boys is my sister's secret boyfriend? I'm supposed to get to know him as a stranger while he plans their next date and plays me for a fool? How is that fair?

An eerie sensation scatters across my shoulders, and I look up to Allie's room. The attic's round window gleams against the sunlight. A dark silhouette obscures the glass, but I can't make out specific features. A hard mass forms in my throat. I climb on the rock and squint. By the time the sun disappears behind a cloud, the window is empty.

I don't know who Allie's secret boyfriend is, but I know who I don't want him to be. And that jealous, intrusive thought scares me more than the beast prowling in the woods.

14

THE ROOT OF THE PROBLEM

"*T*oday, we're going to pick ingredients for the quarterly S&S project." Miss Deveraux slams a big green volume on her desk. "I'll expect each team to come up with an extensive list of all the spells, enchantments, and potions related to their given ingredient. You'll pick a basic spell to practice and demonstrate next week in front of your peers, then an intermediate, then a challenging, and so on until you're stuck. If you can't get past challenging, you'll fail the class."

"What if we fail the class?" Olson asks with a pale face.

"Once you're out, you're out." Her gaze meets mine. "Yes, that goes for the new recruits, too. If you can't keep up with your peers, there's no point in keeping you here."

It's like she knows what happened yesterday on the field, and I swallow a bitter wave of humiliation.

"Nice pyrotechnics out there," Cole whispers in my left ear.

The hairs at the nape of my neck rise, but I roll my shoulders back and brush off the compliment with a scowl.

"Did I offend you by being born or something?" Cole asks. Amusement and impatience mingle on his breath. The rap of his ringed fingers on the desk present a perfect picture of annoyance. One copper, one brass, one silver, the same as his earrings. I wonder what they mean, if anything.

"The other day, in the library, were you the one who made me slip?" I ask in a harsh whisper.

"And why would I do that?" The neutral mask plastered on his features reveals nothing.

I press my tongue against the roof of my mouth. "To humiliate me."

"I don't have to play tricks to humiliate you. You manage that all by yourself."

"Fuck you, Cole."

"Watch your language, or Miss Deveraux will make you wash your mouth with black soap."

Flynn snickers from his seat across the aisle. "Like soap could make her clean. She's always going to be a dirty mortal."

I ignore both of them and examine the possible ingredients for the project. They are separated by level of difficulty, and I immediately know I want to pick one in the hardest category. That'll show Deveraux how serious I am, and that I never back down from a challenge.

"We should choose one of the three most difficult ones," I say with my best commanding tone.

"No."

I crane my neck around to glare at my partner.

He leans over me so he can read over my shoulder, and his breath flutters down my neck. "Deveraux always does this. She tricks you into thinking she'll respect you for picking a harder one, but it's a ruse. These four," he motions to the top column, to the ingredients listed as intermediate.

His long fingers brush mine.

I yank my hand off the parchment.

"These four are actually the most challenging picks, because they are used in the most potent spells in existence. Mind control, matter transfiguration, elemental mastery, and advanced medicine."

I gape and check his assessment. My teeth grit together. He's right.

We go back and forth on which one is the best, but Flynn and Melanie beat us to the punch. The bloody thorn turns red on our list as Miss Deveraux approves their choice.

Cole and I exchange a glance, and he nods.

We need to secure the second-best choice, so I scribble the name on a piece of parchment and hop off my seat. I whizz around Jeremy and beat him to the teacher's desk.

Okay, I might have pushed him. A little.

Miss Deveraux' red-painted lips quirk up. "Demeter's roots. Nice pick. Now, get started on that first spell."

Jeremy groans behind me and turns on his heels.

The satisfied arch of Cole's brow fills me with a misplaced sense of pride.

"Good job getting in front of the wolf," he whispers.

I grumble an acknowledgment. I can't forget that we were at each other's throats a minute ago.

A dozen basic spells associated with our pick are listed on the paper Deveraux handed me, and I peruse the choices thoughtfully.

When I throw the first ingredients into my cauldron, Cole sighs. "You know, we're supposed to be a team."

I smack his hand away from my cauldron. "I'll manage without you, thanks."

His nostrils flare like I've just slapped his face. I tense up at the violence in his eyes, thinking he might retaliate, but he just grabs a fist of his hair. The legs of his stool screech loudly as he slides away and puts a good foot of space between us.

Good. This way, I can concentrate.

We both work in silence, a fitting job since I chose that exact spell to practice. Five minutes before the class ends, Cole gather his things and walks off without saying goodbye.

"Julia. A word," Deveraux calls as the students hustle out.

My spine straightens immediately.

"I'll wait for you," Lydia mouths silently before she slips out.

I play with the hem of my skirt and wait for the teacher to speak.

Her red sequinned sash bristles against her thigh. "Your father told me you're interested in becoming a High Magus."

"Err—yes."

She sifts through the stack of papers in her hands. "You won't succeed."

"Excuse me?" The last thing I need is another small minded teacher that has it out for mortals. Deveraux is instrumental to my success here, and the weight of her next words might crush me, so I brace myself on the desk. My fingers turn white over the wood.

Her gaze flicks to my hands before she meets mine head on. "With your attitude, failure is unavoidable. High sorcery isn't for hot-tempered witches. Fire might be your element, but instead of mastering it, you're letting it govern your life. You got paired up with one of my best students, and you're too busy bickering with him to realize how much he can teach you."

My jaw slacks.

"I know he doesn't come across as a straight-A type, but Cole is a natural. Stop fighting with him. Watch him. Learn. Or you'll wash out like so many students who thought they were above teamwork."

A tinge of shame pulses inside my chest, but my first instinct is to defend myself. "He's an ass."

"He's a young Fae prince. Of course he's an ass. High Magus use their enemies' weaknesses to their advantage; they don't whine about it."

I nod, knowing anything that comes out of my mouth now will only earn me detention.

That damn prince has everyone under his charm, even Miss Deveraux.

I drag out of class. Mr. Oz is standing in the hallway.

He pushes himself off the wall when I approach. "Julia? I sent Lydia ahead. Can I speak with you?"

"Sure." Another depressing teacher pep talk might be all I need to spontaneously combust.

"Dr. Chen gave me your testimony. I'm responsible for the security on Academy grounds, and I have a few questions." He reaches gently for my cauldron's handle.

"Oh." I let him take it, and my sore arm applauds his gallantry. Those suckers are too heavy.

"First, can you show me exactly where you were when you saw the yellow eyes?"

"Of course."

We walk to the spot where the monster spooked me. The gnarly trees look almost friendly in the daylight. A potent thunderstorm erased the paw prints that I saw.

He scribbles something in his notepad. "You say you ran when you heard the growl?"

"Yes. I was alone and freaked out. There were weird paw prints in the mud right here." I point to the exact spot.

A feather tucked in his mouth, Oz crouches down to examine the ground. He passes his hand over the wet soil and casts a spell. The earth forms a vague animal-shaped print.

"Why were you late to the party?" he asks.

"Lydia and I were stuck on dish duty."

The corner of his mouth quirks up. "The dreaded dishes chore. And you saw the anomaly around 10:15 pm?"

"Yes."

"Did you see Holly at the party?"

I look to the ground. "No, I didn't know her. Is she okay?"

"She's still in a coma. Her roommate says she left the party early, around the time that you arrived. Can you make a list of every student you saw when you got there? You can give it to me tomorrow."

My breath quickens. Does he have a suspect in mind?

Oz's gray eyes carve into me like a knife. "Anything else that could help us catch whoever did this?"

I swallow hard.

"I'm going to be straight with you here, Julia. A lot of people, students and staff combined, weren't happy with the Council's decision to allow mortals to return to the Academy. This might be an isolated incident, but…"

"There was a shadow," I blurt out.

A dark cloud obscures his chiseled face, and he rubs his jaw. "A shadow?"

"Yes. It was huge, with tendrils and a darker, blurry area that looked like a mouth."

Oz's previously inquisitive expression wrinkles into a deep frown. "Be careful, Julia. Shadows of that sort come from the underworld. And if a demon acquired your scent…he'll be coming back for seconds."

My mouth slacks. "A demon?"

The third realm is the most mysterious of the three. The Underworld is a place few mortals ever live to recount, full of monsters that sometimes bleed into our reality. Witches have the ability to harness the powers of the demons that live there, that's why we have such an affinity for elemental magic, but we never, ever wish to meet our dark patrons. Summoning a demon into our realm requires immense power. Whoever did this means business.

Oz pats my shoulder. "Don't tell anyone else for now. I don't want to cause mass hysteria over nothing. If there's a demon here, I'll find his trail."

15

LIBRARY THINGS

"*D*emeter's roots." I whisper.

The thick reference books at the front of the library fans through the pages until it reaches its destination. The volume settles on a blank page that writes itself faster than my eyes can read, the paper now filled with book names and stacks on where to find them. My breath stutters. There are at least 30 books with references to the plant. I'm going to miss dinner.

I start with the book about the witches of Dark Falls, the one I forgot to check out last time, and gather a few others on Demeter's roots. Many volumes are listed as restricted.

Flipping pages, I delay the inevitable, but I know I'll have to ask the librarian, Mrs. Pembrooke, about it.

Her purple stare narrows behind her lizard-print glasses, and she looks about as happy to see me as a pixie failing her flying permit. "Miss Winslow. How can I help you?"

I hand her my meticulous list. "A few of these books are in the restricted section?"

Her frown eases somewhat. "You want a pass for the basement? There's one left, but with your…particular skills, I think it'd be best if I bounded your powers first."

With a wince, I extend my arms and place my hands palm up in front of me. Dad used to bind my powers all the time when I was little, but it's been a while.

I hate it. The spell that restricts my fire magic is painful and dangerous. If I let the heat build too much while I'm bound, I faint like a rock heading straight for the bottom of the ocean.

Of course, with my stunt from the other day, Mrs. Pembrooke will not let me visit the most revered collection of books without a foolproof fire extinguisher.

"You can only open the books I approved from your list. Nothing else, otherwise you'll be sorry, and you'll be banned from the library for the rest of the quarter."

I nod in understanding, hop down the stairs, and follow the corridor searching for the right section.

The long, rickety stacks tower above me. They are filled with precious, ancient, and especially dangerous volumes. Black magic and arcane spells sprinkle these halls. Secrets are stocked away in these leather-bound beauties, and the perfume of dust and deceit pervades the air. My blood runs wild. I don't exactly know which spells guard the collection, but everyone in the three realms has heard of this place.

The stone wall is cold under my fingers, and I head down the right stack only to find a small table tucked between two rows of books.

Cole is sitting at that table, his notebook open in front of him.

My breath hitches. "You're here." I pat my blazer's pockets, but there's no salt left in them. Why don't I have any salt?

"We have the same assignment. Of course, I'm here." His grin is cocky yet secretive. The dim lights of the torches light his face with a warm orange glow. He removes his bag from the table and sets it on the ground like he's making space for me.

Out there, surrounded by people, I can handle him. I brush off his Fae charm and his mind-numbing beauty. I ignore how his arms fill the school's uniform better than any of the other guys.

But this is new. Different. There is no one around to buffer our words. No witnesses.

Gods! It's stuffy in here.

I shake off my blazer and plop it on the back of the chair across from him. If I leave now, he'll know it's because of him, so I have no choice but to carry on. I inventory the pile of books already on the table and search for the ones he hasn't already found.

The narrow ladder creaks when I align it with the right stack. With a grunt, I stand on the tips of my toes and grab one of the slimmest reference books.

"Be careful up there. Wouldn't want you to get hurt again." Cole steadies the ladder, and his hand rests about an inch from my foot.

I force a deep, cleansing breath out of my lungs.

"Went a little nuts on the tattoos, Sabrina?"

I grip the ladder tight. "What tattoos?"

"No need to lie. I can see them through your shirt."

My tongue presses against the roof of my mouth. "I don't have tattoos." Is he trying to distract me so he can spook me with one spell or another and make me fall?

I hurry to solid ground, but Cole gives me barely an inch of space. He points to my shoulder, and I follow his gaze.

A black mark smears my skin from my shoulder blade to my neck. My stomach cramps. All previous suspicions are tackled by a healthy dose of what the fuck. "What—what are they?" My neck hurts from my efforts to look over my shoulder, but I can't see.

Cole's warm hand peels the cotton from my lower back, and his fingertips brush my skin.

A molten heat rises in my belly, and I freeze. "Get your hands off me." The words come out breathless, barely louder than a whisper.

"Shush. Let me see them." He drags the shirt up until my back is bare to him. The fabric hugs the lace of my bra on the sides.

I tremble, my mind running laps. This has got to be a trick, right?

"They're ancient Fae runes. They must have been activated by a spell." He doesn't sound sly, but genuinely curious.

A nervous hiccup pops out of my mouth. "You did this!"

"I swear I didn't." He sounds sincere.

Whatever Mrs. Pembrooke did to me wasn't so harmless. "What do they say?"

"My ancient Fae is rusty. Give me a minute."

Four hot pressure-points explore my back like it's a treasure map, and I'm literally melting from the inside out.

My head pounds, and I bite my bottom lip hard to keep from moaning when Cole unhooks my bra.

How sad is it that this is the most sensual moment of my life? Maybe if it wasn't, if I was more accustomed to a man's hand traveling down my body like he wants to remember every groove, I'd be able to keep a cool head.

Wake up, Jules. He's making a move on you.

But I can't stop it. I'm transfixed by the caress of his hand on my shoulder blade. The cold metal of his rings contrast with my boiling-hot skin and drives me mad. Cole leans closer, and the movement sends a cloud of his spicy, leathery scent into my nose.

He reaches my hairline, and my head bends forward. The sensitive skin tingles in delight. A bead of sweat trickles down the valley between my breasts.

Cole traces a rune shaped like an infinity sign, then runs his fingers down my spine. "It's a different page on this side."

Maybe I'm allowed to lose my head.

I've got a Fae prince *reading* me.

Fists curled at my side, I wait for him to lift up my skirt, squeeze my ass, or sneak a hand to my front. I fully expect him to make good on his reputation.

I hold my breath when he gets to the hem of fabric at my lower back.

This is it.

I'm still undecided about what to do.

What I should do is shove him off.

What I want is muddier.

I don't want to lose control. I don't want my first sexual adventure to go around the rumor mill in less than a day or for everyone to accuse me of being another Fae groupie.

I hate to put that much power into Cole's hands, mainly the power to hurt me.

A guy who apparently *collects* virginities.

That thought tips the scale heavily in favor of a violent resolution, but he's still reading, and his hands stay firmly inside the lines.

He's mind-fucking me with courtesy. The lingering suspense makes me question which hand will stray, which path his sinful fingers will choose.

But he has to be working up to it, right?

According to everybody, sex is his middle name. I've seen him kiss at least four girls since I've been here.

Why isn't he copping a feel already?

"It's some type of binding spell," he announces, his voice steady and calm like he's staring at a piece of paper and not at all aroused or bothered by the crackling heat that's threatening to floor me.

"What?" My mouth is pasty, my brain fragmented by his touch.

"These." He skims my left shoulder blade. "They're similar to the ones we get when we're young so we don't kill anybody by accident."

"But those..." his thumb glides down the slope of my neck. "Those are peculiar. Like a curse, written in reverse, but it's incomplete. The ink fades right there." His hand presses into my waist. The tips of his fingers sneak an inch below the hem of my skirt right above my hip bone before he pulls away. "They're fading fast. You should show them to Dr. Chen."

The shirt falls to my hips and seals both my fears and hopes.

"No, thanks. She'll quarantine me or something." I spin around and cross my arms to hide the disgraceful, unhooked-bra look. I can't ask him to redo it, and I lack the confidence to do it myself. Fumbling with the three little hooks in front of a Fae prince is not acceptable.

This is a nightmare.

Cole returns to his seat so fast I miss most of his movement. "Did you ever go to Faerie?"

My eyes narrow. "Of course not."

"Hey, it's an honest question. You're the one with an ancient Fae curse written across her back."

"There must be a simple explanation. Pembrooke bound my powers, maybe she overdid it."

He arches a brow that both insults me from being so naive and challenges me to admit I don't believe my own words. "Pembrooke is no Fae."

"I've noticed."

We're still talking, great.

Why is my stomach sinking like a stone inside my belly? Why is it bad that he didn't try to use me for sex? Why should it reflect badly on me?

Maybe he's not as much of a womanizer as everybody implied.

Maybe he's just not that into me...He doesn't want to fuck an ugly mortal.

Why does it matter? I would have shoved him off anyway.

I tuck my hair behind my ears. "Thank you, I guess."

"Wow, I'd never thought I'd hear those words coming from your mouth. You're awfully rude, you know."

The haze recedes. "Rude?!"

"You accuse me of bullying you and then play the ice princess, even after I caught your mistake."

My back stiffens. "A mistake I never would have made if not for you."

"How is your mistake my fault?" Amusement bubbles in his voice, like he's perfectly aware of the effects his glamor has on me and would find nothing more delightful than to hear me say the words out loud.

"You called me a dirty mortal."

"Flynn said those words, not me."

Ugly mortal then, don't you remember? I want to scream the words, but I can't show him his speech from the other day still affects me. "Do you always play with semantics?"

The corners of his mouth curl up. "I'm a Fae."

Somewhere between the witty repartees, this has started to feel like flirting.

"See? You're the one who's been acting like a jackass," I say.

A mind-numbing, electric smile spreads on his lips. "Let's agree to disagree."

Why are you giddy? Stop feeling giddy!

But the thrill pulsating across my abdomen can't be tamed back into reason.

He pushes a pile of books toward me. "You look through these four, and I'll take the rest. Between the two of us, we can probably finish by dinner."

"Okay."

Cole's pen flies over a blank piece of parchment, his brows bent in concentration.

I discreetly step behind the stack to avoid a wardrobe malfunction and rearrange my bra. Once everything is back in its rightful place, I sit in front of him. He's consumed by what he's doing. His amber gaze travels across the book, his elbow propped on the table. One hand scratches an absent-minded pattern behind his ear.

In a weird way, I'm seeing him for the first time, seeing the man behind the Fae glamor. A sharp intelligence is hidden behind the princely smugness. The dark stubble on his chin roughs up his smooth, creamy skin and makes him look more human.

Unfortunately, the tameness of the quasi-absent Fae glamor isn't the turn-off I thought it would be.

16

HOMEWORK

When I return to my room, Lydia is hunched over a thick red book and a piece of parchment, scribbling notes.

"What happened to you? I thought we'd eat dinner together?" I throw my leather bag on my bed. The standing mirror in the corner of the room shows me no trace of the weird rune tattoos, and I let out a breath of relief.

Lydia grunts. "Sorry, I have an essay to write for tomorrow, and with Divination at 7:00, I had to power through."

I peek over her shoulder. "You're writing an essay on Fae ancestry?"

"Yep. It's my punishment for missing the History of Magic class. Blane and Bailey trapped me in Miss Eillis' shed, and it took forever to get out. I have to do a family tree and everything."

My fists curl. "Those snakes need to be put in their place."

"Don't anger them; it'll only fuel their idea that this is a game."

I rap my fingers against the back of her chair. "Why the Fae?"

She plays with a lock of red hair absent-mindedly. "Miss Black put me up to it. Do you know they used to abduct mortals and use them as slaves? And that some of them still do? It's disturbing."

"I thought it was illegal to keep slaves now."

"In theory. But if you make a deal, they own you. They can argue that you technically agreed. Fae deals are unbreakable. If you go back on your word, you waste away and die a slow death."

My stomach curls. "Creepy. No wonder my father warned me copiously about Fae deals."

Lydia's fingers skim the red leather of her grimoire. "It says here the previous Fae King had a harem of 30 women and men. Who needs that much sex?"

"Fae, apparently." A harem sounds about right.

"Look, Cole is even listed here." She points to the top of the tree, where a big, gnarly branch separates into a dozen more. "He's the thirteenth offspring of King Kirkan, but it doesn't mean he won't get to rule. Fae Kings rule for a thousand years, after which they choose their successors amongst their living children."

A thousand years...no wonder they're in no hurry to graduate. Four years is like a drop of water in the large bucket of quasi-eternal life.

"What about the queen?" I ask.

"There is no *queen*. There are *queens*. Kirkan is married to eight women."

I draw in a quick breath. "Girls everywhere are throwing themselves at royalty."

Lydia throws me a sideways glance. "And you wouldn't join them, given the chance?"

My eyes narrow. "Would you?"

"Maybe. I mean—Flynn is a tool, but Cole is not nearly as brazen. He looks shy."

I muffle a snigger into my palm. "Shy?"

"Okay, not shy. I don't know...mysterious. You can't tell what's going on behind those gorgeous amber eyes of his."

That, I have to agree with.

"I don't think he's that handsome," I lie, pushed by whatever happened earlier to distance myself from this conversation. From Cole. Lydia's great, but I haven't put her loyalty to the test yet. I know from human middle school that, if you ever admit a crush to a new girlfriend, you've got to be prepared to own up to it.

Lydia tilts her head to the side and raises a brow. "Come on, girl. It's only me and you here. He's interested in you."

Fire swirls in my blood. "He's not."

"Get real, Jules. You have a nice figure, and your rebel vibe is like honey to guys like that."

"I have a rebel vibe?"

"Don't change the subject. What are you going to do about this? A Fae prince. Aren't you curious? Remember the card." She reaches for her tarot deck.

I cover her hand with mine. "I do remember. I remember the prostrate woman chained to the tree. Fooling around with a Fae is stupid and dangerous."

"If you say so." She backs off, but I'm rattled.

My chest is tight and my breathing ragged. "Do you know if Holly got out of the infirmary yet?"

"Vivianne told me she's still unconscious. If she doesn't wake up soon, they'll transfer her to the General."

My mouth opens in shock. Non-magic humans deal with a ton of illnesses, but we don't. Magic can fix everything from a broken knee to a fractured skull. As long as you're found alive, a practiced Healer can cure you. If they can't, you're sent to the only hospital in the realm. The General Care Center for Magic Ailments and Curses.

This hospital is usually reserved for the Magisterium agents wounded on duty, not a student on her way back from a party.

I think back to Oz's demon theory and shiver.

Leaving Lydia to her paper, I gather everything I need for my upcoming class, throw a jacket over my shoulders and find a nice spot in the gardens to study.

Fog billows in iridescent clouds over the warm earth, the air thick with humidity.

After about an hour, a dark silhouette slices the white, powdery air and startles me. I jump to my feet.

"Hey, are you in late-night Herbology, too?" Trent asks. The school jacket looks good on him. I never saw him wear it before.

I press a hand to my breast and force my muscles to relax. "Nope. I'm just looking for a quiet spot."

He stands right next to me and stares out at the night. "Good thing I showed up early." His angular jaw is almost blue in the moonlight.

I follow his cheekbones to his thick eyelashes. "Your eyes are really dark tonight."

"I'm overdue for fresh blood."

My sneakers crunch the gravel of the path.

A light chuckle erupts into the night air, and Trent buries his hands deep in his pockets. "Don't worry, I won't attack you. I've got plenty of blood bags in my refrigerator." His gaze follows the slope of my neck. "Unless you're offering."

I laugh nervously. "I'd rather not."

Like it's the most natural thing, he catches my hand in his and plays with my fingers. "You're a virgin, aren't you?"

"Err—what?"

"You've never been bitten."

I cough into my hand. "Right. No, never."

"It's as good as they say…" He licks his lips, and a hint of white catches my eye.

I can't help but stare at his pointy fangs and swallow hard. His palm travels up my arm until it rests in the crook of my neck. A shudder slices right through me.

"I'd give anything to be your first," he whispers so close to my face that his cold breath frosts over my cheek.

"I'll keep that in mind." I don't know if I should be flattered or disgusted by the raw need rolling off his tongue. If we were talking about sex, I'd tell him off, but vampire customs are very intense when it comes to blood. This might be one instance where cultural differences added to Trent's tendency for boisterous comments are muddled, so I play it off as a joke. But my heart beats faster and faster, and a fire builds in my belly, hidden by my jacket.

Drop-dead gorgeous Fae, smoldering vampires... This school is full of landmines.

17

HUNGER

*D*ivination is on the West Tower's roof, and the cloudy night's sky rumbles above our heads. Lydia, Allie, and I huddle on one of the ten king-sized cushions. The soft, blue velvet under my palm sends goosebumps up my arms.

The six-foot-three teacher is incredibly attractive. Melanie warned us that his classes have become a flirt-a-thon. When teachers barely look older than students, crushes are bound to bloom. The horse shifter has a square jaw and bright blue eyes. The fitted black blazer and matching tie give off a stern executive vibe while his tanned skin, checkered undershirt, and wild brown hair warms the look with a cowboy twist.

The round roof is surrounded by stone walls and turrets. A beautiful, perfectly transparent glass dome protects us from the wind.

Pixies giggle out front. Sprites play with each other's hair on the right.

The few boys that were brave enough to join us glower from the back. Olson is with them, holding his knees to his chest, and when our gazes cross, we both nod in greeting. He pries a pen and post-it from his bag and scribbles a few words. The yellow square appears in my lap a second later.

Can we talk after this?

With a brow arched in question, I throw him another glance and nod.

Jessa skips over to the boy cluster and sprawls in the middle. Olson's eyes widen, and he runs his fingers against the shaved side of his head.

"What the hell?" I mouth silently.

But my mortal friend is now entranced by the sight of Jessa's short skirt and plunging cleavage.

Mr. Brady claps his hands together. "Star reading won't be possible tonight, I'm afraid. We'll settle for something else. Who can list the various tools a seer uses to make his or her predictions?"

He closes in on us, and his gaze settles on Lydia.

"What's your name, sweetheart?" On any other professor, the sugary tone would sound creepy, but since this one is a cross between an Olympic swimmer and a teenage heartthrob, I swear nothing that comes out of his mouth ever sounds creepy to a female ear.

My roommate squirms. "Lydia."

He draws in a sharp intake of breath. "Lydia Hawks... It's an honor." He shakes her hand for too long before he catches himself.

She clears her throat loudly. "Predictions can be based on something as trivial as a twig moving against the wind, but the most common tools used are cards, tea leaves, stars, palms, dreams, and the infamous crystal ball."

Mr. Brady's mouth stretches into a blinding smile. "Now, who can tell me why those methods aren't as accurate as a star reading?"

"The reading is only as flimsy as the vessel." Jessa's dry but melodic voice cuts through my eardrums.

"Good work, Jessa."

I crane my neck around. Her harem is still fixated on her. One of the shifters, Jamison, is massaging her feet. Olson looks transfixed, and I roll my eyes.

Allie elbows my side. "I hate that girl." The venom in her hushed voice takes me by surprise.

I brush it aside on the count that I wholeheartedly feel the same way.

By the end of the class, I'm not sure I made the right decision picking this course. Divination is so fluid. Imprecise. Everyone is tripping over themselves to please Mr. Brady. I gather my things.

"Lydia. Can you stay behind?" Mr. Brady asks.

Lydia's eyes bulge.

Allie hugs me goodnight. "I'm beat. I'll see you tomorrow."

I hang back awkwardly, standing right in front of the door leading back inside the tower staircase, and wait for Lydia.

Mr. Brady sits on his desk and braces his hand in his lap. "Your grandmother was a mentor of mine. I'm so sorry she died so young."

"We all miss her." Lydia wraps her arms around her frame.

Brady combs his brown locks away from his tall forehead. "She was an amazing woman. Do you know what happened to her tarot deck?"

Lines appear on my roommate's forehead. "I have it."

Mr. Brady scratches his neck. "Here? In school? I figured you'd keep it under lock and key."

"Are you going to steal it from me?" she laughs nervously.

"Of course not. But others might." He pats her shoulders for an instant. "Good job today."

The enigmatic warning hangs in the air, and Lydia inches toward me, stunned.

"What was that about?" I ask.

Her rosy cheeks are proof that Mr. Brady is even more stunning up close. "No clue."

Olson is waiting at the bottom of the stairs, but he's not alone. Jessa leans on the stone wall, her creamy leg propped behind her.

My eyes narrow.

Olson bounces from one foot to the other. "Hey. I wanted to talk to you. Holly woke up."

"Did she say what attacked her?" I ask.

Olson kicks a small rock at his feet. "She couldn't remember."

A cruel chuckle pops out of Jessa's big mouth. "The mortal woke up and ran for the hills. She dropped out the second she was able to put two words together." She licks her lips. "One down..." The evil grin stuck on her face makes my fist itch, but she pushes herself off the wall and struts away.

I give Olson my best what-the-fuck-are-you-doing-with-her look.

He raises his hands to the sky. "Hey, I'm not stupid. I know she wants something from me. My dad is on the student housing committee. She's not the first to ask for a private room."

"You're not going to help her, right?" I ask.

A wicked glint warms his eyes. "Of course. She's hot."

I smack his arm.

He sobers up, his carefree face darker than I've ever seen it. "Listen. We're all thinking the same thing. Someone on campus isn't happy with our presence here. We have to be careful. Especially you."

I cross my arms. "Why *especially me?*"

"You know..." His shifty gaze jerks back and forth between Lydia and me. "If you keep angering them, you'll end up with more than a cut, and we'll all be put on curfew. My dad told me about the crap they have in store if we keep popping up at the infirmary. If there's another attack, they might suspend us altogether."

Fire rises up my neck and sparks against my hair. "That's preposterous."

Olson nods. "Yep. Doesn't make it less true. It's all politics and risk assessment with these people. If we want to stay, we have to prove we can take care of ourselves. Holly hurt us by quitting. Now, they all think we're going to bail at the first sign of trouble."

"She was *attacked,*" Lydia says.

Olson shrugs. "So what? This world isn't for the faint of heart."

From Lydia's frown, I get that she disagrees with Olson's simplistic view of our position.

We all walk together out of the forest and back onto the main path. Olson waves goodbye in front of his dorm.

When we arrive at Summer Hall, the crescent moon is high in the sky. The leaves are quiet, the air pleasant, and I toss my jacket over my shoulder.

"Did you see the look Jessa gave me when Mr. Brady asked to see me after class?" Lydia asks with a quiet grunt.

"No." To be honest, I'd made an effort not to look at the Fae after seeing her beam from the boys' attention.

"I swear, she hates me as much as she hates you."

I let my fingers brush the leafy bushes on either side of us. "She hates all mortals who aren't obsessed with worshiping her."

"Speaking of worship…" Lydia elbows me in the side and nods to the Victorian house towering against the night sky.

The porch light is on, and a dark silhouette is sprawled on the steps. I instantly recognize Trent's form. He's looking up at the sky, his eyes closed to the moon like he's getting a tan.

The vampire hops to his feet as we draw near and stretches gingerly.

Lydia hides her smirk with her palm. "I'll see you later."

I open my mouth to protest, but she's already gone.

Trent's eyes are still crimson, and the knowledge that he waited for me, hungry, is enough to quake my whole body. He's no longer the goofy, approachable vampire.

"I had to see you. I couldn't stop thinking about our last conversation," he says in a throaty whisper.

"Err—I'm still not—"

Cold lips brush mine and the fresh taste of cloves invades my mouth. He keeps it soft and languid, and I moan. His polite but expert tongue teases me with the promise of so much more.

He presses his forehead to mine. "I'll go now, but don't forget my offer."

The pad of his thumb presses into my jugular for a brief second. The vein bounces to life under his touch, and my pulse hammers harder with each breath. A pressing urge to throw my head back and offer myself to him radiates down my spine.

"You were built for this," he breathes, clearly drinking in my reaction. "One of these days, I'll sink my teeth inside that beautiful neck of yours, and you'll beg for more."

His hand holds my throat, and my lids flutter. Fear swirls in my blood, but it's drizzled with curiosity. Truth be told, I don't doubt his assessment one bit.

18

NAKED

"We're late for S&S." Lydia's vigorous push shakes me awake.

The remnants of sleep blur my vision as I grab my uniform in the drawer and yank it on. My sluggish pulse escalates into a fanfare. Deveraux is known to lock out students who are late.

The weekend came and went too quickly. Since it's early in the quarter, many students went home, so Lydia and I got acquainted with our fellow mortal friends. A few of them are immortal groupies, but most of us have a solid head on our shoulders and are already plotting to get this stupid mortal seminar canceled.

Ten people is not a lot of elbow grease for a mutiny, but if we can get under Mr. Wright's skin, we might be able to at least get a new teacher—one that doesn't believe short skirts are reason enough for murder.

Lydia and I run down the hill to the main building, our bags in one hand, our cauldrons in the other. My knotty hair flies around my face since I didn't get a chance to tame it into a braid or a bun. This early time slot is a bitch, but I'm sure I set that alarm last night.

"How come the alarm didn't ring?" Hands braced on my knees, I catch my breath by the entrance of the classroom and check the time.

We're still three minutes early, and Deveraux isn't here yet. Thank the Gods.

Lydia shakes her head. "No idea."

I eye Blane and Bailey suspiciously. After the stunt they pulled on Lydia last week, I know they enjoy messing with mortals.

"Hey, Winslow," Trent greets me.

"Hi." I stop by his desk in the second row. My spot out front is currently occupied by Naomi. The pixie is flirting with Cole, so I can spare a minute. I rest my heavy cauldron on the ground.

The vampire passes a nervous hand through his brown locks. "I'm sorry for the other night. I didn't want to come off as a creep. We vampires are a bit intense, especially when we're hungry."

"You're fine," I wave dismissively.

He arches a playful brow. "So you'll go out with me next Saturday?"

"I didn't say that."

"Come on. What do I have to do? We have Duel tomorrow. I'll beat up Flynn just for you."

I laugh like he's being silly but touch his arm playfully, the universal signal for chase me, I'm interested.

Deveraux's shadow appears in the doorway, and I pick up my cauldron and carry it to my desk. I've been practicing my silence spell all weekend. Only half the students will be evaluated today, the other half on Thursday, but there's no way to know which half will be first. Teams are pitted against one another. If both teammates manage to cast their spell successfully, the best team receives an A, and the others a C.

Naomi is still sitting in my spot. Her blond hair falls in perfect ringlets around her face, and I comb my fingers through my hair, trying to smooth down the mess.

She paws my teammate's arm to the point of groping him and giggles. To my surprise, Cole is not welcoming the attention. Despite the fact that her pink, push-up bra is clearly visible through her shirt, her breasts all but spilling to the desk, Cole looks like he is about to shove her off the stool.

He curls a fist over his knee, but his angry gaze latches on to me and his knuckles somewhat relax. "Hey."

I dump my bag on my desk.

Naomi cranes her neck around and reluctantly peels herself from my spot.

The nasty glare she throws my way sparks an itch in my shoulder blades, and I wonder if the pixie isn't the one who disabled our alarm to get some face time with the Fae prince.

Cole throws his head back and groans. "I shouldn't have kissed her. I'm not into her at all, and now she follows me around everywhere."

"Then why did you?" My eyes widen at the unusual exchange.

He buries his head in his book.

"Morning. I hope you're all ready to work." Deveraux strolls up to the front and sends random flares to the students that will perform today. The spell creates puffs of red, blue, gold, or green over the chosen teams. Cole and I get nothing, and my stomachs sinks. I would have loved to get the assignment out of the way today.

Blane and Naomi are first, and the pair demonstrates a transmutation spell by turning Lydia's necklace into a frog.

My knuckles clench. Every project is another opportunity for them to pick on us mortals.

When Flynn prowls to the front of the class, I know I'm next.

"Mel and I chose a vanishing spell." He rubs his hands together like a cartoon villain.

"What will you make disappear, Mr. Verinos?" Deveraux asks.

Flynn's perfectly straight teeth form the imitation of a smile. Wickedness dances in his eyes. "You'll see."

Then, I feel it.

I'm...bare.

Under my skirt, my underwear has poofed out of existence. Legs crossed, I freeze. My nails dig into the desk and leave crescent marks in the wood.

Miss Deveraux raises a brow. "So?"

The evil glare latches on to me. "Ask Julie."

A vengeful snarl curls my lips.

Deveraux sighs like she knows exactly what's going on. "Alright. *Julia?*" She enunciates my name to set the record straight, but Flynn clearly called me Julie on purpose.

Can I lie here? Probably not.

With a smug grin, Flynn reaches for my skirt.

I hop to my feet and hold an arm out to stop him.

"Flynn, if you would make the item reappear," Deveraux orders with a sharp, uncompromising tone.

The bastard reaches into his jacket and pulls out a big pair of stained, white cotton briefs and whistles. "Eighteen going on eighty."

Laughter echoes around the class. Blane and Bailey pound on their desks, Brie sneers, and Lydia is a human tomato. Trent narrows his eyes at Flynn.

A sickening heat flushes my face. "That's not mine."

Flynn nods in agreement and tosses the ugly piece of clothing into the trash. "No, you have sluttier taste. Take note, boys. Julie is so desperate for it, she's always prepared." He extends his hand, my lacy black thong hanging from his crooked finger.

The wheels of my brain spin. A basic vanishing spell needs previous preparation. Flynn had to see and touch my underwear prior to this moment, which means he was either in my room or…

I crane my neck around to Naomi and Krystel. Both twins exude a profound satisfaction, and their ugly grins burst with pride. I remember how I grabbed the first underwear on top since I was in such a hurry. They messed with our alarm.

I lunge forward to snatch the fabric from Flynn's hand, but at the last second, he throws it to Cole. The prince catches it in mid-air, his eyes dark.

The laughter doubles.

I open my palm and raise a brow. I'm not going to reach for them again like a moron only for Cole to hold them out of reach above his head. The bastard is tall.

"Why don't you just leave them with him? We all know who makes you wet, mortal," Flynn snickers.

"Enough with the crude comments, Flynn." Miss Deveraux chastises. "This is still my class, not another place for you to show off. Now, sit down, and we can continue without your twisted sense of showmanship."

Cole's throat bobs, but he hands me back my underwear.

They all expect me to run for cover and put it back on, but I won't give Flynn the satisfaction. Instead, I cram them in my blazer's pocket and sit.

Miss Deveraux throws me an impressed nod and turns to Flynn's teammate. "Melanie?"

The vampire cocks her hip to the side, and her black flat taps the floor. "Well, I should make Flynn's dick disappear, but we all know his personality is the real problem."

Flynn leans over his desk, arms propped beneath him, and gives her a sly smile. "We all know you could never hurt my dick, Mel."

Behind him, Trent stands up abruptly. "Stop fucking with my sister."

Flynn rolls his eyes. "If only she'd stop fucking me."

Trent leaps forward and throws a right hook at Flynn's jaw. The desk slides a few feet in my direction. I jump to my feet and retreat towards the wall. Trent throws another punch, his biceps straining. The Fae ducks out of reach, but the vampire circles him, fast as lightning. The commotion of their swift, muscular bodies creates an empty circle around them as everyone tries to stay out of the fray.

Inching backwards, I collide with Cole's chest. My breathing hitches, and I rush forward to correct my mistake, but his hand grips my hip. His steel grasp holds me out of harm's way when Flynn all but collapses onto my stool. A flash of blond hair and a trail of blood whirl into my vision, inches from my face.

Trent's nostrils are huge. His chest rises and falls quickly, his muscles bunched. The sinister look on his face makes me gulp, and I pray never to be on the receiving end of his anger. His red eyes are all but spurting fire as he lands another kick in the middle of Flynn's chest.

The cocky Fae falls to his ass, laughing. Blood trickles down his mouth, and his palms raise in surrender.

Deveraux's eyes are murderous. A force field shimmers in the air between the two brawlers. When Trent goes for Flynn again, the vampire stumbles to the ground like he was just tased with a high voltage stun gun.

Cole's hand dips lower and settles on my thigh, right below the hem of my skirt. I want to move or shove him off, but my head is spinning.

Deveraux taps her gold sequin heel to the floor. "Mr. Darkwood, report to the headmistress' office. Physical violence is not tolerated in my class."

"Whatever." Trent spits at Flynn and storms out.

"You too, Flynn. I warned you about the language," she adds.

"Alright." Flynn peels himself off the floor. He gathers the blood at the corner of his mouth and licks it off his thumb with a wink. "I'll see you and your underwear later, Julie," he boasts in my direction before he heads out.

Arms crossed over my chest, I skirt around the broken stool and away from Cole.

The class returns to Melanie's spell, but my ears are buzzing. I can still feel each of Cole's fingers pressing on my thigh, and I'm still not wearing underwear. All the righteous humiliation from before mixes with the weird, smothering heat that snaked around me as surely as his hand did. I'm fighting for breath, perched on my stool. A pulse lances between my legs, and I can't find a comfortable position.

When Deveraux excuses us, I bolt out of the classroom. There's a bathroom directly in the corner. I disappear into the first stall, sit atop the closed lid and force my sweaty hands to stay on my knees.

The water turns on. I peek through the crack next to the bolt and grab my thong from my pocket.

Melanie washes her hands at the sink. "Damn Trent had to be the hero again," she says.

"He stood up for you." I wrangle the underwear past my flats and pull it on like armor.

The row of mirrors reflects only my presence when I come out of the stall and join Melanie by the sinks. "Why do you sleep with Flynn? He's an ass." My judgment comes off even worse in the face of my body's reaction to Cole's proximity.

Melanie tilts her head to the side. "He's not so bad. Besides, all the boys in this school are beasts. I prefer one with its claws on display instead of the ones that masquerade as sheep. It keeps it real."

My crotch starts to itch. An unfamiliar, painful burn travels up my thighs, and it's got nothing to do with arousal. My heart sinks. I'm such a naive girl.

I tear the underwear off and dump it into the nearest trashcan, but it's too late.

"Property of Cole Desirys" is etched into my skin. The words are written over and over in small red calligraphy. My ass, sides, and upper thighs are literally branded with his name.

Melanie arches a brow at my tantrum, and I inch the fabric of my skirt down to show her my hipbone.

She bends over and breaks into a fit of giggles. The sound scratches my ears before she wipes the tears from her eyes. "He got you good. You can get back at him on Thursday."

"Flynn or Cole?" There's no way to know which one is responsible for those marks. Flynn is the one who had my underwear the longest, but it's Cole's name that's tattooed into my flesh.

Melanie waves dismissively. "Flynn probably put Cole up to it. It's not about you, don't worry. You're fresh meat, and those two love to sample the female menu and fight for first pick. They love to compete."

The words are breezy, but her face is tense, and I wonder if she might feel more for Flynn than she lets on. Despite her laughter, she doesn't look pleased by this stunt one bit, and I detect a hint of steel in her voice.

19

BEST LAID PLANS

"*I* am not going with you to a slumber party. Besides, I'm supposed to study tonight." Hands firmly planted on my laptop's keyboard, I avoid Lydia's inquisitive gaze.

The loud zipping sound of her duffel bag sends a chill to my neck.

"It's not a slumber party. It's an official field trip with Mr. Brady. Since the woods are off limits for now, we'll observe the meteor shower there. It's worth five bonus points on the exam. I thought you wanted to make top three." She pauses and squints. "Unless you already have plans?"

Heat creeps on my cheeks. My seer roommate sniffs out secrets better than a bloodhound.

Rain drips along the turret's windows, and I point to the one closest to me. "The weather sucks."

"The forecast is good for the night. There should be plenty of stars to examine," she chimes happily.

I should know better than to use the weather as an excuse.

Two weeks have passed since the S&S debacle, and while Cole and I aced our basic and intermediate spells, the challenging one is proving to be a bitch. After thong-gate, he'd been incredibly subdued. The first few days, I'd found it suspicious, but now...

115

We work well together, and lately, our study sessions haven't sucked so bad. I don't want Lydia to know I'm supposed to meet him tonight because she'll give me that look—the one with her red L-shaped brow and knowing smirk. I feel naked when she serves me that look.

The redhead shakes her head. "Come on. It's better than passing out in front of your laptop screen."

I open my mouth, but I can't think of a good reason not to go. Damn it!

She grins, both brows rising in the air, her chin tucked up. "You're meeting Cole tonight."

That seer is a mind reader, and I'm so busted. "Yes," I admit.

"Finally, some honesty! Girl, I was starting to think you were icing me out."

"No, I just—I'm still not sure how I feel about him."

"It's okay. I've got your back, Jules. But I need you there tonight, or these girls are going to eat me alive. Now, go tell that damn beautiful prince that you're coming with me. You get bonus points and you play hard to get. Win-win."

I chuckle and start packing. Those five points are worth the aggravation of a night out, especially if Lydia needs me.

She follows me to the library. The stairs are wet with rain, but the sky is clearer by the second.

"I'll be just a sec," I say.

Lydia adjusts the strap of her overnight bag and leans against the stone banister. "Uh-uh."

"Julia Winslow," I speak quickly to the guard.

The gargoyle huffs when I rush past him, but I've got to hurry.

I could have sent Cole a note, but the library was on the way to the West Tower. And I wanted to see him.

He's at our spot, one foot firmly planted on the bottom step of a ladder. His tall frame and long arms allow him to reach the top of the stack without much effort, and he slides a thick, black volume back into place. His blazer is spread over the back of his chair, and the white, form-fitting undershirt hikes up his chest enough to reveal an inch of skin.

The restricted section has become somewhat of a sanctuary. He's different here than out there. I can't quite explain why, but he's cocky instead of smug, and the difference matters.

My heart tumbles at the light in his eyes when he sees me coming.

He jumps to the ground. "You're early."

I point to the blue overnight bag tucked under my arm. "I'm leaving."

He grabs the shelve above my head and leans in. "You're ditching me for Mr. Brady?"

There's something dark in his gaze that prevents me from laughing at his logic, and I swallow hard. Truth is: I'm bummed. I was looking forward to tonight.

He raps his knuckles over the book spines. There's a long, drawn-out pause at the end of which he tugs at the tip of his pointy ear. "Okay, if we can't do it tonight, come to me tomorrow." If I didn't know better, I'd say he's disappointed.

"Which dorm are you in?" I ask.

His eyes widen like I've turned into a green extraterrestrial. "You don't know where my house is?" His shoulders hitch underneath the crisp, white uniform. "I don't live in a dorm. The rooms are minuscule."

The sudden urge to yank his tie down and choke him is almost undeniable. "We can just meet here."

"We have two days to blow Miss Deveraux's socks off with this spell. Our entire grade depends on it. Now, we can either cram into the library on a Sunday night with everyone else—which means Flynn too—or endure your roommate's incessant babbling. Secret option number three, we can concentrate and work at my house. We'll be completely alone. I don't see why you're being difficult."

"I'm not—" My mind is stuck at *completely alone.*

A slow grin spreads on his mouth. "I'll see you a seven. Don't knock. Send a flare to the East window, and I'll open the door for you."

My tongue sticks to the roof of my mouth. "I still don't know where you live."

"You'll figure it out." He taps the stack above my head before sitting back in his chair.

I turn on my heels and hustle out.

Lydia is sitting on the steps outside. Her hand travels fast over a sheet or parchment as she sketches the gargoyle with a small piece of charcoal. The creature's chest is slightly puffed like he's posing for her.

"Where does Cole live?" I ask.

She ties her sketchbook back shut and returns it to her bag. "I don't know. With Flynn in Winter Hall?"

I miss a step. "You know where Flynn lives?"

My roommate turns bright red. "I might have heard it mentioned."

To my knowledge, all the houses on campus are dorms...unless Cole lives in Faerie. No, he wouldn't have invited me there. I've been around the Academy a lot these past few weeks, and I have no idea where Cole might live.

"He invited me 'to his house'. To study."

"Of course." Lydia nods emphatically before she breaks and snorts into her hand.

I smack her shoulder but follow suit. I'm not naive or delusional. Cole Desirys doesn't invite girls to his house to study, and I'm weirdly okay with that. It's stupid and vain, but it's the first real sign that he might not find me ugly at all, and my chest is both too tight and too warm to entertain the thought for long.

No, I know why he invited me over, and I'm going to go regardless.

I've never been a coward, and that prince's tie needs yanking.

20

PILLOW FIGHTS

*T*he Divination excursion goes according to plan until we get into our tents. Allie, Lydia and I end up with Vivianne and Tammy—a pink-haired beauty that looks more like a Care Bear than a shifter.

We're rooming with the cheerleaders…so to speak.

There's no team, but there's enough pep and school spirit in the air to nauseate me. Matching gold pajamas shimmer under the bright spot above our heads, and I think I found the Academy's equivalent to a sorority. Lydia is clearly a better fit than me since she seems to be quite caught up with the school's gossip. Next thing you know, she'll volunteer to braid their hair.

"Where's Jessa?" Tammy asks when she comes back from the bathroom, a small cabin up the hill from where we made camp.

Vivianne rolls her eyes and rubs lotion into her face. "She said she wouldn't sleep in our tent because she didn't want to catch anything from the mortals."

Tammy pops her bubble gum loudly. "Ugh. She's a total bitch."

I watch the panther shifter with more interest. She's taller than all of us by a good foot, and her long legs seem to be in her way as she

119

shuffles around to get comfortable. She's the only one who's got a dark comforter like me instead of a pastel one.

"You're just jealous," Vivianne chimes.

"Fucking jealous. She can go to hell with her perfect blue hair, porcelain doll face, and size-zero waist. The boys are all drooling over her. It's Jessa this and Jessa that."

Vi's eyes soften, and she pats her friend's hand. "Fred dumped you for her again, huh?"

Tammy's shoulders drop. "That panther is lucky that my parents want me to marry a pure-blood shifter, or else..."

I bite my tongue and jerk a glance at Lydia, knowing she'll cover the bases.

"I thought Jessa was with Cole..." my loyal roommate trails off.

Vi scoffs. "Fae, especially at that age, aren't known to be monogamous."

The girls settle under the covers and adjust their pillows. The magic light dims above our heads. It's cozy, so we all have to fight for a space, but the floor is cushy and totally unnatural. This tent must have a built-in spell that makes it as fluffy as a king-sized mattress.

I pinch Lydia's arm.

She shakes her head no.

I kick her shin through the covers.

"Erm—where does Cole live?" she finally says.

Vivianne sits, hugging her knees, and bounces her eyebrow up and down. "Why, you interested?"

Lydia shrugs. "I'm curious."

"He's crazy selective. If you want some Fae-loving, you better ask Flynn."

Lydia's chest flushes with a deep red blush. "I don't—"

Tammy rolls over to her side. "It's okay. Flynn's got a great body, and his cock is—"

"Tammy!" Vi yelps.

The girls giggle. I'm smack dab in the middle of Operation High-School Flashback.

The tall shifter shrugs. "Hey, a girl has got to live. Fae sex is something to check off the bucket list."

"Flynn is fine, but I'd love to get that prince naked." Vi raps her manicured fingers over her mouth.

Tammy shakes her head. "Then turn back time. Flynn told me that Cole is into virgins. You qualify, Lydia?"

My roommate shifts next to me. "No."

"Then Flynn it is. I can give you a few tips…"

I hug the duvet to my chest, squirming at the TMI turn the conversation has taken, and pry my water bottle from my bag.

Vivianne's garnet eyes bear into me. "What about you, Winslow?"

"Huh?"

"You're paired up with him in S&S. I've heard he's very talented with his mouth…"

I choke on my water.

"I heard Winslow is busy with a certain vampire…" Tammy trails off.

Vi's eyes widen. "Melanie will tear your head off, girl. Nobody's good enough for Trent, especially not…" She stops herself and drops her gaze to the ground, a nervous hand playing with her side braid.

I stare at the ceiling and grit my teeth. "Say it. Especially not a mortal."

"Their father is the richest man in this realm. I'm sorry, but—"

"We just kissed. It's not like he proposed," I snap.

"What about you, Allie? We know you're getting busy. Who's the lucky guy?" Vi asks.

"I don't know what you're talking about." Allie meets my gaze and pokes me with her toes.

She doesn't want them to know, and I give her a slight nod. I won't sell her out to the Cheer Brigade, but I'd still appreciate if she would come clean to me.

"I need to pee." I wrestle my way out of the covers and zip the tent back behind me.

The chill of the night bites into my face, and I'm grateful for the heat spell Mr. Brady cast over all our tents. The boys are on the opposite side of the clearing, and the light is already off in the third tent.

The moon is bright, and I easily follow the path up the hill to the cabin.

On my way down, a high, needy cry tickles my ears, and I flatten myself to a tree. Someone's in the forest. The glass bottle containing the silence spell I brought with me in case one of the girls snored is heavy in my pocket. I cast it on my boots and slowly travel toward the sound. At first, I'm thinking about the demon and Holly's attack, but the nature of the moans become clearer and clearer, and my ears heat up.

Two people are having sex against a tree. I catch a glimpse of the girl's naked thighs, wrapped around one fine male ass. The guy's pants are bunched at his feet.

Jessa's blue waves are unmistakable. They are loose and fall to her lower back. A few strands stick to the bark at her back. The man is also easily recognizable, and my jaw clenches. A hot wave of disappointment and disgust chokes me.

Mr. Brady is like every other hot-blooded male in this damn school. Sex and power. That's all everyone here cares about.

I hurry back to the tent and hide my face in the pillow. The girls have quieted down, and I force my mind to think about anything but the rapture on Jessa's face.

IN THE MORNING, Lydia and I walk to the small cabin to wash up. Fog licks the cold earth, and dew frosts over the blades of grass. The spiky ends crunch underneath our boots. The water is freezing, and we quickly brush our teeth and tame our hair into a semi-decent state.

When we step over the stone threshold to return to our friends, a cold wave washes over me. "What the fuck?"

Magic slime—what we call the leftovers from our cauldrons after the spells are used or bottled—cascades across my back. The icy goo sticks to my eyes, ears, and nostrils.

Its putrid smell makes me gag, and I furiously wipe down my face, fighting to catch my breath. My ribcage constricts in disgust.

"Now, they smell like the filth that they are," Jessa chimes.

The other girls are wrapped in a half circle around her. A few of them laugh, a few hug their chest, but none of them, not one, comes to help.

Tears stream down Lydia's face, her knees shaking.

I leap down the small hill and punch Jessa right in the face. To my extreme satisfaction, she goes down like a rock. Her perfectly shaped nose spurts blood, her legs scampering beneath her to return to a standing position. She trips and falls on her ass. The long, slick strands of blue hair stick out in all directions, and a red bruise blossoms on her right cheekbone.

I spit a mouthful of slime at her and let my fire build.

Jessa sends an electric jolt my way, but my sister's element is air, so I've got quite a bit of experience in avoiding lightning strikes. I duck and send a fireball directly at Jessa's legs. The skin of her calf singes and blisters under my hardened stare. I want to do so much more than nick her precious leg.

I clasp my neck, looking for my necklace, and my eyes widen. It's not there. Fire rises tenfold, and the small crowd that had started to form around us steps back.

"You took my necklace! Give it back!" Hell hath no fury like a woman who's been stripped of her mother's only heirloom.

Jessa shuffles to her feet. "I couldn't be less interested in your green rock."

"Give it back!" A nasty fireball billows in my hand, and I inch forward. The image of Jessa's face melted by fire sings a wicked song inside my bones.

Hard fingers close around my arm. Flynn is there, wearing all black, his blond, almost translucent hair hidden underneath a black beanie. "Get your hands off her!"

I try to yank myself away from his grasp, but he's too strong. He's not in this class, and I realize he must have been the one to bring the slime. "It's all fun and games until we fight back, isn't it?"

Sharp nails dig into my skin. "You should be back in Faerie, polishing our floors." He grabs a fist of my hair and tugs. His Fae magic slithers in every fiber of my being.

A kick at the back of my knees makes me waiver. They want to break my skull and dance over my corpse. I see it in the harsh set of Flynn's brows, in the storm of hate rolling deep inside his crystal-blue eyes. I feel it in the hard bunch of his arms.

"Nobody move!" Mr. Brady's voice isn't sugary or seductive. It's all steel, and he stands taller than usual. The scene freezes, Flynn's fingers still digging into my hair. The teacher strolls toward us. "What happened here?"

"The mortal punched me," Jessa whines, holding her face.

Mr. Brady's eyes flash with anger.

I'm fucked. He's boning the girl I just punched.

But his cold stare flicks to Lydia, and his gray eyes soften. He watches his lover with a sad frown. "You did this, didn't you?"

"I—I" Jessa stutters, her eyes wide.

The other students are all here now, staring. Allie looks grim among them, her arms wrapped around her red Academy jacket.

"Flynn. Detention for a week," Mr. Brady barks at the tall Fae. "Jessa and Julia...pack up your stuff. You'll be meeting the head-mistress at three."

"But—" Jessa's voice breaks, a crack wide enough for tears to flood in, and I watch her with newfound interest. Maybe she's not just fucking the teacher. Maybe she likes him.

Mr. Brady's jaw is tight, his teeth clenched hard enough to pulverize diamonds. "I don't want to hear it. If you so much as brush each other again, you'll be suspended pending a formal investigation."

The shifter trots off like he's about to burst into a horse and stomp on us all.

"You're lucky he intervened," Flynn seethes, inches from my face. His hot breath reeks of the same spicy scent as Cole.

"What were you going to do? Drown me in insults?" It's dangerous to poke a bear, but I want to fillet Flynn until he's in tears, and I've never felt that way before. It stings. The bitterness at the back of my throat pulses every time I look at him.

Energy sparks off his hand, but he buries it in his black hoodie. "We can pick this up in Duel. I want a rematch."

"I'll tear your face off."

"It'll be my pleasure to send you to your grave, mortal. And the first one who yields has to quit the class." He extends his hand.

"You're on." As soon as the words leave my mouth, I know I messed up. I'm too proud to go back on a bet, but I need Duel to become a Magus. My skin screams in revulsion as we shake hands.

This was a pretty stupid bet to take, especially when Flynn beat me last time we faced each other, but that was weeks ago.

I'm prepared now; I can make him bleed.

And boy do I want to wipe that smirk off his face and see a bruise mar his perfect Fae skin.

21

THE DEVIL WEARS A TIARA

old eyes. Calculating gaze. Hateful vibe.

Celeste Draco is terribly beautiful, but her aquiline nose and piercing gaze aren't exactly inviting. Her short black hair finishes right above her pointy ears. The mid-night blue pantsuit hugs her lean arms like a second skin. She clearly doesn't eat, but she doesn't look frail.

I squirm in my seat and hold her hollow stare. Her office is at the back of the house and has its own entrance. I wonder why the head-mistress wouldn't keep her office near the administration only to remember the woman in front of me isn't your typical headmistress.

She's Fae.

A Fae queen—a fact that is made crystal-clear by the intricate jade, silver, and diamond tiara sitting on her head.

She is also Cole's mother. Fae wives don't take their husbands' surname, and I remember Dad mentioned the Dracos once or twice over the years. Jillian Draco is the High Council's treasurer, and her sister rules Dark Falls. No wonder they're such a powerful family.

I bet she gets to do whatever the hell she wants. Like her son. Who lives here...

She wets her red-painted lips impossibly slowly. The disdain in her voice betrays a hint of recognition as she reads Mr. Brady's note. "Julia Winslow. Why am I not surprised?" Hands twined over her desk, she jerks a glance to the Fae sitting next to me. "Jessa. What happened?"

"She punched me," Jessa says through her teeth.

"You attacked us," I seethe.

Jessa brings a hypocritic hand to her breast and opens her mouth like I said the most shocking lie. "Attack? It was just a hazing ritual. All in good fun."

I imitate her congenial tone. "Fireballs are fun, too."

Cole's mother holds up one terribly intimidating finger. "Shush."

I grab both my knees not to punch the fake-ass innocence from Jessa's face.

"You can go, Jessa," Celeste says.

My enemy skips out with a satisfied grin.

Celeste continues the staring contest until I blink. "Here, at Dark Falls, we don't punch other ladies in the face." There's something quiet about her scolding voice that chills me to the bone. "Do you understand?"

I bite the insides of my cheeks hard, scared to open my mouth and say something that'll get me expelled.

"Now, I know you witches don't have a lot of time to learn the ways of the world, but if you expect to stay in my school, you won't pull a stunt like that again." The condescension slices through me. She flicks me away with her hand. "That's all."

"I need to go to the bathroom," I say, curious to see more of the house before I go, still undecided if I should return later and meet Cole like he asked.

If Celeste caught me with her son, that'd be awkward. Or it'd be amazing to see the horror on her face...

Celeste clicks her tongue. "Upstairs. First door on the right."

The ground floor is a Home and Garden darling. Ceramic, quartz, and porcelain. Not at all what I expected a Fae house to be, but it's also sterile. Cold. I rub the chill off my arms and head out toward the main entrance, crossing the kitchen and the living room. A staircase stands right out front, and I climb it quietly. The plush carpet squishes under my flats.

A door is ajar on my left, and I risk a glance through the crack. Cole's school bag hangs from a chair in front of a cluttered desk.

The hinges screech as I push the door open wider.

A white, embedded fireplace casts an orange glow over his king-sized bed. Gold lines made to look like roots are etched into the head-board. The sheets are hidden by a stark red duvet with black stitching. A lavish fur from a Faerie tiger is sprawled at the base. The white, blue, and black hairs are soft under my touch, but my heart breaks for the tiger. Hunting animals for sport must be big in Faerie.

A piece of parchment is pinned on a board over the desk, and the names immediately catch my eye. Julia Winslow. Allie Winslow. Lydia Hawks. Olson Lewis. Holly's name is crossed out in black, my name is circled, and a question mark stands after Allie's. My nose wrinkles.

Why would Cole keep a list of the mortal students above his desk?

A pot of ink stands next to a glass of muddied water, and a piece of paper sticks out of a book in his opened bag. I push aside the cover to take a peak, and the drawing inside knocks the wind out of me.

Runes are written along the woman's bare back. Luscious dark hair falls over her shoulder, and the ink shimmers with a peculiarly warm light.

Cole drew me. He tried to recreate what he saw in the library and scribbled notes in the margins. That or he's the one who put the runes on me in the first place, but that seems like a big leap.

Fae alphabet runs across the page at the bottom. I snap a picture with my phone so I can translate them later and find out if the prince is making a fool out of me or not.

The stairs creak loudly, so I whiz out of the room, cross to the bathroom and close the door behind me. Sweat gathers on my fore-head, the porcelain sink cold against my hands. I press on the flush to keep up appearances in case the footsteps I heard were Cole's and wash my hands, drying them with a hand towel that is disgustingly soft and expensive.

When I come out, the hallway is empty and Cole's door is still ajar.

I hurry down the stairs and into the cool air of the sunny December afternoon.

Cole was certainly not upstairs because he's here, at the foot of the hill on which his house is perched.

He's got one arm wrapped around Krystel's shoulder. He holds her close to him and whispers in her ear the way he does with every damn girl. The pixie giggles as they separate, and he climbs up the trail to his house.

I can't avoid him, so I roll my shoulders back and continue walking.

The mischievous smile falls from his face. "Sabrina...we said seven."

I hike up my bag's strap over my shoulder. "I'm leaving. I've had enough Fae drama for one day."

"This isn't—" A cloud obscures his face before he wets his lips. "We still have to work on our spell."

The shrug I serve him is 30% so what and 70% I don't give a fuck. "Have a good night."

I'm not surprised. Cole is the type of guy to double book his evening. It shouldn't affect me. If I'd come on time, if the mess with Jessa hadn't happened, I might have seen his bedroom for more than a minute. I might have joined the ranks of the hundred girls he's kissed. For a fleeting, eerily beautiful moment, I might have believed that he sees me as something more than a willing female.

Instead, I get to walk away with my dignity and pride and a possible clue to this whole shadow-rune fiasco.

No sex, but I can hold my head high.

That's my life. My choice.

My damn virgin destiny.

22

GRAVITY

The library is crawling with students when I rush in after dinner. It's Sunday, so everyone's scrambling to catch up with the work they procrastinated over during the weekend. Now that Cole and I aren't working together, or doing anything together, I'll have to pull an all-nighter.

S&S first.

Cole's notes on my weird tattoos last.

That's the plan anyway, but I keep glancing at the language section, wondering how long it takes to translate three lines of Fae text into something semi-readable. It's not like there's a Google translator for Fae alphabet—not that I would use a damn translator to decide if I should trust a Fae prince.

The Fae dictionary is as thick as my waist. The cover glistens with green and gold Faerie ink, and the subtleties of the graceful swirly lines that make up the letters is not only foreign but completely dumbfounding. This is going to take forever. Since my patience is already wearing thin, I decide to do the next best thing. Using a fresh pen and ink, I recreate Cole's note to a T on a new piece of parchment.

I wait for the change of shift and corner the night librarian—with all the nocturnal creatures attending night classes, the library never sleeps.

Mr. Hoggs is a small vampire with long gray hair and a tired face. The deep lines around his eyes seem to indicate that he's as old as most of the books on display. He never speaks much. The disdain he clearly feels toward us students is a plus in favor of him keeping my secret. The fact that he's not a citizen of Faerie helps, too, in case Cole's note is compromising.

"Hello, Mr. Hoggs." Clutching the piece of parchment, I bounce from one foot to the next and wait for him to acknowledge my presence.

"Hello, Mademoiselle Julia Winslow."

He always says my name like that, slowly, completely, like a perfectionist French sloth. Rumors say he was the curator of the Louvre museum back when it first opened.

"I've come across a Fae passage relating to my research, but I need someone to translate it," I say.

He hikes his minuscule round glasses up his tiny nose. "Why don't you ask a fellow student?"

"Faerie folks don't like mortals much. I'm afraid they'll translate it wrong." I make my eyes as big as I can.

"I will translate the words for you, then." He hunches over my offering. "Hmm."

"Is it bad?" I eye the dictionary again and wish I'd had the patience to deal with this myself.

"What research did you say this was in reference to?"

I swallow hard. If I tell a clear lie, he might not trust me enough to tell me the truth. "I found this in my Dad's old papers."

His eyes soften for a split second, and I let out a breath of relief.

"It's an ancient Faerie Curse written next to a separate concealing spell." The ominous undertone of his drawl sets my teeth on edge. He pauses before adding, "And this note here at the bottom is quite interesting. It says: does Jules know she's not human?

My head spins like the stacks of books have suddenly caved down on me. "Maybe you read it wrong?"

"I'm perfectly fluent, Mademoiselle Julia Winslow." He cleans his glasses and puts them back in line with his eyes. The carmine irises scan me from head to toe like he's never really looked at me before. "If that is really your name..."

I huff, yank the page away from him, and cram it deep inside my bag. The condescending chuckle that follows my retreat grates at every bit of my pride. Cole must be playing a damn trick on me, because I'm as human as they come. That damn prince is trying to get into my head.

"TODAY, I'm starting at the back of the list. Julia, you're first. Who would you like to challenge?" Oz asks, his trusty Duel notepad at the ready.

This is it. The moment of truth. My eyes search the crowd. "Flynn."

The Fae hops to his feet. "Alright! Let's go!"

The crowd's excited chatter tickles my ears. The bleachers are twice as full today. A lot of students came to see who would win the stupid bet. A throng of "Flynn for the win" signs waft in the wind.

"Mr. Verinos. Please keep your seat. You fought Miss Winslow already," Oz says.

Loud, disappointed groans echo around the sand mounds of the arena.

My jaw slacks. "But— That's not part of the rules."

"It is now." Oz's tone is unequivocal.

My mind reels. If Oz is trying to look out for me, he's not helping. In fact, all the pent-up energy in my body crawls for an out. I have to fight. I have to win. There's no other option to soothe the ache in my bones, this incomparable need to prove myself to these filthy people. I need to flatten a Fae today.

With a dejected frown, Flynn pats Cole forcefully on the back. "Cole. Teach that witch a lesson for me, will you?"

All eyes turn to Cole, and I swear I see a hint of annoyance flicker in his eyes before he rises to his feet.

My mouth dries up. It's not the same. All my confidence pours out of me like blood flowing from a deep wound I didn't know existed. An itch at the back of my head warns me that Cole is the better fighter, that this might change everything.

He hasn't tried to prank me with the rune drawing yet, but it doesn't mean he won't. I let that thought fuel my appetite for violence.

"Cole vs the mortal. Well, we all know who wins this one," Brie snickers. She blows a pink bubble gum, and it snaps at the exact right moment to punctuate her jab.

"My money is on the witch," Melanie shouts from behind her brother, and I smile.

Trent gives me a thumbs up.

Fire warms my fingertips. I wanted to pummel Flynn into oblivion, but I'll have to settle for second-best. A Fae is a Fae.

The dark prince passes his thumb over his lips as we walk toward the center of the arena. "This is so unnecessary. Why did you even take the bet?"

"Afraid to lose, your *majesty*?" I coat the word with a healthy dose of sarcasm.

A cocky smile glazes his lips. "Call me that again."

"Ugh. Let's do this."

He unhooks his cufflinks and rolls the white sleeves of his uniform to his elbows, the muscles in his forearms defined and distracting.

A few feminine whistles boom from the bleachers.

He looks me up and down. "You dressed for the occasion."

My eyes narrow, and I watch his fingers closely, wondering what he's doing. If I hypothetically wore my best black camisole and sexiest leggings for this fight, I'm sure as hell not going to admit it.

"Are we just going to talk?" I steal a glance at the students. They're all whispering between themselves, their eyes riveted on us.

"What else would you rather be doing?" He asks with a lopsided grin that adds insult to injury.

"Fighting. It's a duel class."

He shrugs, hands in his pockets.

If he thinks I won't strike first, he's dead wrong. The fire coils in a tight ball, and I hurl it at Cole's face. He ducks. "You throw like a girl."

"Fight me, you coward!"

A hand covers my eyes, and my mouth opens in surprise.

Fuck. The one in front of me was an illusion, and the real Cole is standing an inch behind me, his breath hot on my ear.

Too close.

Way too close.

"Ask nicely, and I'll consider it." The low baritone of his husky voice resonates like a gong in every fiber of my being. The magic in his words is thick and undeniable.

He rests his chin against my shoulder and motions to our audience. "Deep down, you're just like them. Everyone wants to be us."

The tip of his tongue ghosts over my ear. Adrenaline sparks across my nerves, and I spin around, but my brain short-circuits.

Cole twines our fingers, preventing my next fireball from forming, and my arms fall at my sides.

His gaze slides to my lips, and a sly smile blooms on his face, his dimple playing hide-and-seek with the sunlight. The golden rays highlight his marble-white skin, and my eyes widen in horror. Cole Desirys is leaning in to kiss me in front of the whole class.

And I'm going to let him.

My hands are numb, my gaze unfocused, and I can't move.

He's got me right where he wants me.

What did Mr. Oz say? Don't be afraid to use any and all of your skills. Why use violence when you can rule by temptation?

At the last second, right when our lips are about to brush, he wraps his hand in my hair and pulls my head back and down a few inches.

"Yield. For your own good." His breath is fresh and spicy, drugging me like a high-priced, velvety scotch.

"No," I croak.

His eyes narrow, and he uses his hypnotic voice again. "Then you'll kneel for your prince."

"Fuck you."

White-hot energy spills from his fingers, and my knees soften from the compulsion.

I need to kneel in front of him more than I need to breathe. My entire body shakes as I resist his command, but my soul yearns to submit. I'm merely a puppet, and all my strings have found their master. Bile burns my mouth.

My powers build inside me, and I set a big blast loose. The flames scatter over his shirt, and the fabric catches fire.

Cole meets every ounce of my magic with his Fae shadows. Black and red meet in the middle.

I squint, and Cole does the same.

A sandstorm whirls around us and shields us from view. The fire rages on, my skin immune to my own powers, his apparently resisting the heat.

"You don't think I'd cast a protective spell? You're a one trick pony, Fire Girl. Now, kneel," he shouts over the heavy wind.

His shirt falls to pieces at our feet, and his beautiful, black feathery wings sprawl on each side of him. He's in full Fae form, and my eyes can't contain whatever they are seeing. My salty bubble gum is useless against the iridescent spectacle in front of me. A rainbow of color shimmers underneath his skin, his eyes so bright they're almost gold. Sweat condenses like rain over his bare torso and drips down the ridges of his stomach.

Out of instinct, I grip his hand and bite my tongue hard. Black veins crawl up his arms. I realize I'm covered in them as well, the purple-ish streaks covering my forearms. "You kneel."

We both fall to the dirt at the same time.

The magic wind whips so hard around us, I can barely keep my lids open. A shadow swallows the ground beneath us.

"Your eyes..." His thumb grazes my brow and circles my eye on its way to my cheekbone.

I feel raw. My heart pounds as though I'm wearing my skin

inside out.

A thunderous sound echoes directly above us, and a cold heat scatters all the way to the tip of my toes. A million volts of electricity implode all at once inside my neurons.

Until there's nothing but darkness.

23

FAINT

The bitterness in my mouth stings on its way down. My arms are numb, and my rib cage hurts. Stiff muscles are throwing a pain-party down my legs. My heavy lids work long enough for me to see the faded blue curtains of the infirmary. Scratchy sheets ghost along my chin, and I groan.

The weak sound is barely audible because of all the yelling in the next room.

"She assaulted my son." Celeste Draco's voice borders on shrill.

My eyes snap open. The three beds next to me are empty, and the doors leading to Dr. Chen's office and the private room are shut.

"They were dueling," Mr. Oz explains.

"No one is allowed to use infernal magic at the Academy. Especially not a mortal. It's too volatile," Celeste says.

"The students are encouraged to use any and all of the skills at their disposal."

"This barbaric curriculum of yours might need some Council overview, Professor Osbourne."

I shuffle to my feet. The hospital gown falls at my mid thighs, and I'm naked underneath. The smell of melted Lycra and burnt cotton haunt my nose, my Duel clothes probably in ashes in the middle of the arena.

Fuck. I hope Flynn didn't see me naked.

Dr. Chen's clinical, calculated voice resonates through the empty room. "I welcome any and all Council recommendations."

Celeste snorts. "I want that witch expelled from my school."

"That wouldn't be fair!" Oz shouts.

My stomach sinks. I've done it. I've managed to get kicked out of the Academy before the end of the first quarter.

A loud throat-clearing sound interrupts them both. "It's not your school, Celeste, and my girl is not going anywhere."

Dad! My heart soars and squeezes at the same time. Dad is here, and he's fighting for me. He's referring to the stone-cold headmistress as Celeste. That ice queen deserves to be taken down a peg or two. Just as I'm about to jump up and down with my Go-Dad metaphorical pompoms, my breath catches.

A furious blush pools on my cheeks. Dad was counting on me to do well, and this doesn't qualify. I inch forward, my bare feet sticky on the linoleum, and press my eyes to the crack of light streaming through the door.

Dad is standing in front of the doctor's desk. Celeste isn't visible, and Mr. Oz sits in one of the two chairs opposite Dr. Chen.

"You have no power here, Daniel," Celeste chimes.

"I've got a letter from the President demanding we let this matter go."

I hold my breath. The President of the High Council wrote a letter for me to stay in school? It's fantasy! No way has the President heard of me. Dad doesn't use his position to get favors. Not ever.

Celeste appears next to Dr. Chen and crumples the letter. "She uses those powers again on school grounds, and we'll have to report her to the Magisterium."

The infirmary's door cracks open loudly behind me, and I spin around. My heart pulses like a raw sore inside my chest.

"Jules?" Trent whispers.

I jump and run over to him, my legs still wobbly beneath me.

He wraps an arm around my waist to steady me upright and glares at the hospital gown hanging from my frame. "Are you okay?"

I play nervously with the hem of the fabric. "I think so." Leaning into his embrace, the scent of cloves and pine needles chases away the stink of sweat, fear, and ash.

"I sneaked past the guard," he says.

"There's a guard?"

"Yes. Everybody is whispering that you sold your soul out to a demon to win the bet. What the hell happened earlier? I didn't know you could conjure infernal magic." His cold hand cups my cheek.

The gentle touch soothes my feverish skin, and I press my lips against the inside of his palm. "I didn't know either."

The deep lines in his forehead disappear. "Who won?"

My brows furrow. "Huh?"

"We couldn't see anything. Once the storm cleared, you were both unconscious. Who passed out first?"

My head hurts just thinking about it. "I can't remember. I need—I need to talk to my dad."

Celeste barrels inside our bubble like a reaper coming to collect our souls. Dressed in black from head to toe, she looks paler than death. The tightness of her scowl and the bunch of her fists makes me glad she's not actually holding a scythe.

"You shouldn't be here, Mr. Darkwood," she enunciates slowly.

Trent winces. "I just had to know Jules was okay. I'll go."

Celeste growls and disappears into the private room.

"Is Cole in there?" I ask, suddenly putting two and two together.

Trent nods. "I guess so. You were both completely out of it when they carried you out of the arena."

"Wow." I put the headmistress' son in the infirmary using forbidden magic. I'm royally screwed.

"I should go." Trent gives me a squeeze and a soft kiss before leaving.

The hug causes my bladder to scream bloody murder, and I drag to the bathroom. Quiet voices seep through the wall next to the bowl and turn my stomach upside down. I grab a sheet of toilet paper, mutter a paper-thin spell under my breath, and aim the magic at the wood separating me from Cole's room. A bit of light streams through the enchanted wall square, but they shouldn't notice anything if I keep quiet.

"You humiliated me today, Cole."

I see the outline of Celeste Draco next to the bed until Cole's head obscures it.

"Yes, Ma'am," he says, his voice trembling with emotion.

"To be bested by a *mortal...*" The word is so vile, it's like it's been dunked in oil and dragged in a dump before being set on fire. "Rectify the situation. I don't want to bring your father into this."

"That won't be necessary," Cole says quickly.

His haunted voice scatters icy shivers along my back.

There's a pause. Celeste rests her hand over Cole's, her knuckles twitching. "Alright. I know you'll help me make things right."

Make things right. What does that mean?

I back away from the wall and set the magic free.

When I return to the main room, Dad is sitting on my bed. His gray hair curls behind his ears, and his cape is slightly wrinkled around the collar area. "How are you, Munchkin?"

"I'm okay." I smooth down the deepest bend in the red velvet.

We both jerk a glance at the two closed doors. The walls have ears, and whatever serious discussion we need to have will wait.

"Let's go to your room to change and get you an overnight bag. I'm bringing you girls home for the weekend." He summons a warm pair of boots and wraps his coat around me.

"I'm sorry, Dad," I whisper.

He squeezes my shoulder. "You have nothing to be sorry about. Nothing."

But the students roaming the grounds sing a different tune. Everyone we cross paths with scampers away like I'm a goddamn walking pandemic. Stolen glances and vicious whispers echo at the back of my skull, and from the way Dad's shoulders tense, I know I'm not imagining things. Nuggets of conversation like "She almost killed him," "what a freak," and "just a demon whore" sizzle inside my mind. Everyone clearly thinks I made some type of deal to juice up my powers. I bet I know who I can thank for that rumor.

Droopy strings of honeysuckle sag against the banister in front of Summer Hall.

Naomie and Krystel skirt around us on the terrace. Their fiery stares drill holes into the back of my head. I bet I would've gotten an earful if Dad wasn't here.

Miss Eillis is cooking in the kitchen as we enter, and Dad gives her a small wave. He turns to me. "I'll have a quick chat with Beth while you pack."

It throws me for a loop how Dad addresses my professors by their first name.

I climb up the stairs to my room, trying to shake off the crushing shame that weights on my shoulders. Infernal magic is not only forbidden, it's got an awfully bad rep. Dark Magus use it. Demons. Murderers.

Only the worst scum on Earth and beyond favors this type of all-consuming power, and I summoned it to win a bet.

Stop it! You did nothing wrong. Dad said so himself.

The trickle of hope in my chest shrivels when I open the door. Lydia is cramming her clothes into her big suitcase. Her red-rimmed eyes and frizzy hair send a surge of panic through me.

"Lydia? What's wrong? Why are you packing?"

She drags the back of her hand over her face. Mascara stains darken the sleeve of her uniform. "I'm sorry, Jules. My parents freaked out when they learned you were my roommate. They asked for an immediate transfer and forbade me to speak to you."

My heart gives one painful beat.

Her eyes remain glued on the floorboards between our feet. "It'll die down. These things always do. But for now, if I don't want to end up at MIT after all, I've got to keep my distance. You understand, right?"

My mouth opens and closes on a throaty cry that sounds like a yes and means everything but.

No. I don't understand at all. Some witches can summon infernal magic. It's not unheard of. Why is everyone acting like I suddenly turned into a demon? Lydia can't think I'm responsible for the attack on Holly, but clearly, everyone else does.

I'm the wicked witch of the dorm.

24

NOT OFFICIALLY

*H*ome. It used to be a quaint bungalow in Connecticut or a two-story brownstone in Chicago. Today, it's a high-rise condo on the west coast. The sun reflecting off the sparkling blue ocean through the humongous bay windows is almost blinding after the Autumn drizzle of the Academy. A tall artificial Christmas tree clashes against the beach scenery. Fake snow frosts the tips of its branches. The familiar smells are those of Dad's turkey and the too-clean paint job. Moving around every couple of years reminds you that Spackle walls and creaky stairways are not what makes a family.

Dad is the backbone of ours, so wherever he is, home follows. Yams boil on the granite island cooktop. The hood above it sucks out the Holiday scents with the rumble of a small airplane. Allie is in the shower, so Dad and I are completely alone, away from the commotion of the Academy and free from possible eavesdroppers for the first time since he dropped me off at school.

"How did you manage to convince them to let us out of school early?" I ask.

"You only had two days to go before break, and everyone needed a bit of time to digest the news of your...outburst."

The gears click in my head. "I was suspended, wasn't I?"

"Not officially." Ever the politician, Dad says the words with a lopsided grin.

I take out my frustrations on a piece of buttered bread.

Christmas is obviously not celebrated by everyone at the Academy, but since most supernaturals live amongst humans, it's one of the recognized Holidays. The other ones being the Fae's Solstice in June and the Shifters' bi-annual beast week.

Dad shoots me a peculiar look over his pot. "Why did you take your necklace off, Munchkin?"

"Someone stole it from me." The furrow of his gray brows and the worried curl of his lips accelerate my heart. "Is that why I could summon infernal magic?"

Dad serves himself a glass of port and pours one for me, too.

I arch a brow. "That serious, huh?"

"Jules...The time has come. I need to tell you something, and you've got to listen carefully until the end."

I nod, my heart fluttering in my chest.

"Munchkin...Your mother wasn't human."

The words split open my heart, my brain, my fucking identity. The note from Cole comes to mind, and how convinced I was that he was playing a trick on me. Despite my absent mother, I didn't even second guess it. I was sure he was playing me for a fool. Clearly, I'm worse than a fool. I'm a fraud.

There's chaos in the silence that follows, and Dad has never looked so tired—or so guilty—in his entire life.

"Err—No, you always said—" Denying it seems like a necessity.

"I lied, honey. To protect you."

I swallow the roil in my stomach, my throat painfully tight, my legs numb. "Why?"

The corners of his mouth curl down. "It's complicated."

Each tear rolling down my cheeks costs me more than the last. "Is she alive? Did you lie about that, too?"

"No. I would never...She wasn't from this realm. Everything I told you about her was true, apart from who she was."

I scoff, blood draining from my face. "I can't be half-Fae. That's not—"

Dad grimaces like my hypothesis tastes worse than a foul lemon. "No. She was from the the third realm. The Underworld."

"I— But— No— Are you saying my mother was a demon?" The unspeakable words grate my throat.

"She was a Fury."

Fury. As in vengeance demon. As in murderer. I've heard the stories, the crimes these creatures commit on their quest for violence and retribution.

My mouth hangs open on a silent wail. No. I must be asleep or drugged. This is all a terrible mistake.

Dad wraps both his hands around mine. "No one can know. Not ever. You wouldn't be safe. You'd have to quit school and live a life in the shadows. I thought I'd bound the magic you inherited from her for good, but something has set it loose. Your necklace was an additional precaution. Did something happen to you at school? Something that could have awakened your mother's heritage?"

I almost kissed a Fae Prince. What about that, Dad?

But I don't mention Cole at all. Or the runes, or the fact that he knows I'm not human. Instead, I say, "Those bitches stole my necklace, and Duel class was the first time I really pushed my magic since then." I clear my throat, my heart beating loudly at my temples, my palms sweaty as hell.

This can't be.

Dad's hands twitch over mine. "After I married Piper, the Council sent me on an undercover mission to spy on a ring of demon slavers. Your mother was the daughter of the man I was spying on. She was beautiful and strong. Just like you. She was funny and fearless, but there was darkness in her—like in all of us. You see, time flows differently in the underworld. When I left for my mission, I didn't know Piper was pregnant with Allie. People think I was gone for a year, but to me, it was ten. It doesn't excuse anything, I know. I went back on my wedding vows either way, but I couldn't tell Piper why. How all these years took a toll...and I fell in love with someone else."

I grip his hands, speechless. No matter how angry or sad I feel about him lying to me all these years, I've never doubted that Dad loves Allie and me.

The wrinkles in his forehead deepen, and his eyes search mine. "After your mother died, I brought you home. I wanted to tell you about her before you left for the Academy, but then I figured it would only make you feel lonely and different. Can you forgive me?"

"Of course," I croak.

I'm not dumb, just shell-shocked. Dad hid this from me for a reason. If the Fae hate mortals, everyone is scared shitless of demons. If people knew, I'd have to live in hiding for the rest of my life.

"Is there any way people could find out the truth about me?"

"No. It's not like there's magical genetic testing. You're still my girl, still a mortal. Your mother aged the same way we do, but her blood makes you more powerful. As long as you don't tell anyone, people will believe that you're either a talented witch or a demon worshiper. Considering half our people can call upon infernal magic like it's Chinese takeout, no one will think twice about it."

Half our people...the rotten half.

I swallow hard, my head bent. My dark mane falls over my face and shields me from Dad. "But it still could get me expelled from the Academy."

He nods. "I'm proud of you, Munchkin. No matter what they say, anyone but you would have caused a lot more damage with an infernal burst of this size. You did well, and you taught that royal prick a lesson."

My arms fall at my sides. The butterflies in my stomach scramble at how dangerous Dad's voice sounds when he mentions Cole.

"Daniel Osbourne told me about the girl that was attacked. Did you know her?" he asks.

"No." I don't have the headspace to care about Holly right now.

I know Dad is keeping me grounded with his questions so I don't throw a tantrum and slam a door in his face. And I hate that it's working. "I cannot believe you lied to me."

"Half of my job is choosing which secret should be buried and which should be shared. Things are not going to get easier at Dark Falls. The Magisterium must have an agent investigating this attack. Another violent act might have terrible consequences."

"Are they going to put us on a curfew?" I ask.

"Where did you hear that?"

From the worried curve of his brow, I figure Olson's intel was right on the money.

"Celeste Draco is going to use her position as Headmistress to retaliate against mortals, that's for sure. The thought that you're in the same class as her son... You keep your distance from that boy, munchkin. If he's half as dangerous as his mother, he might be the one behind the attacks."

Allie drags over to us, a towel wrapped around her head. "She's not just in his class. He's her S&S partner."

My eyes bulge, and the betrayal stings deep in the pit of my belly.

"This is unacceptable." Dad paces the room, the yams forgotten, his knuckles white. He pulls and tugs at his hair like tearing it out of his head will make all the Fae disappear from this realm. "I'm not taking you back there. The place is too dangerous. Pairing you up with a Fae prince. These people have lost their minds."

The adrenaline from before melts into a trickle of fear that slithers all the way up through my tight chest. "What about your fight for equality?"

"Being given the same opportunities as immortals does not mean you should be forced to collaborate with a Fae. I know all their tricks. How they use their beauty to further their sinister plots and belittle us into submission. My daughters will not be toyed with by a Draco. Never!"

In pure worried father fashion, his haunted tone paints a clear picture of exactly how he fears we might be toyed with. I sink my nails into my palms for my fire not to betray how close he is to the truth. How close I came to ruin.

I force the balls of my feet to the ground and uncross my arms. "You're right. We won't."

"Munchkin?"

"We'll show them we're better than them. That their tricks do not work on us." I lift my chin up and convey as much determination as I can muster. "You can't expect me to scamper home with my tail tucked between my legs. That's not who we are."

He grins at my outburst. "You might have your mother's eyes, but you're my daughter through and through."

The pride in his voice warms my heart, even though I'm furious with him, even though I'm skirting the truth. Even though I fear I'm not as strong as I need to be.

Allie inches forward and rests her head on Dad's shoulder. For the first time since she left for school, she looks exactly like the girl I knew.

The tears on her face prompt me to twine our fingers.

Dad wraps an arm around her. "Why are you crying, Peanut?"

"Sometimes, I wish things could go back to the way they used to be," she says softly.

"What do you mean?" Dad asks.

"It's just—Real life is next, you know. There's no use pretending we can all go back to pyjama Sundays and shelter ourselves from these immortals. Now, we have to fight for power."

Dad backs away to meet Allie's eyes. "Power?"

She raises her chin to look at him. "Isn't that what Mom says? That power is better than promises."

I hold my breath. Allie almost never mentions her mother to us. Piper McKinney is a leader for the opposing party, often making speeches on television about all the things Dad is doing wrong. I know they talk sometimes, but not often enough for Allie to forgive her. Unless something changed.

Dad twirls one of her curls around his finger. "Your mother is angry."

"I know, but that doesn't mean she's wrong about everything." With that, Allie waves goodbye. The click of her doorknob resonates through the silent house.

Dad frowns. "Is your sister alright?"

The teenage instinct to stick up for her and ease Dad's suspicions kicks in. Allie sold me out earlier, but I can't do the same. I can't give Dad another reason to keep us out of school. "Of course. You know her, she's just upset that you had to intervene on my behalf. She hates that we don't get to fend for ourselves."

"She's always been fiercely independent. I think you both get that from me," Dad says, finally returning to his cooking.

I watch Allie's closed door and wonder what it's going to take for her to open up to me. "I'll keep an eye out for her. I promise."

25

FRACTURED

*S*ummer Hall is different upon my return. The round room is
half empty, Lydia's bed stripped to the mattress. A thin film
of dust on her desk twinkles under the sunlight that streams through
the small rectangular windows. One drawer of her dresser is slightly
open, and I peek inside to see if she forgot anything. The wood creaks
when I pull it forward.

A piece of paper is stuck in the wedge between the front and lower
panels, probably crammed there in a hurry given the wrinkled
corners. I unfold the note.

I'm still thinking about our kiss.

Damn. Lydia has a secret boyfriend, too. The handwriting is unfamiliar, though. I tuck the paper inside my planner and sneak out the
back door to avoid the pixies.

Since I don't want to chat with Cole or endure any of Flynn's
remarks, I show up for S&S at the last possible second.

By chance or the most fucked up fate, Cole had the same idea, and
we come face to face in the main building's stairwell.

I scan him up and down.

Aside from a slight burn on the back of his hand, he looks flawless.

The crisp black undershirt molds to his upper chest, his jacket nowhere to be found. A red tie hangs, undone, around his neck.

"You're not as roughed up as they implied," I say.

"Well, you're not that powerful, are you?" His hand twitches, and he rolls his shoulders back, the movement deliberate if not a little forced.

Immediately, the change is glaring. Whether it's the tightness of his jaw or the stiffness of his spine, this isn't the Cole I've been studying with for the past few weeks. I wet my lips and choose my words carefully. "I'm powerful enough that your mother accused me of assault."

His hand flies to the burn on his knuckles before he catches himself and tugs down his sleeve. "Don't flatter yourself, Sabrina."

Somehow, we're now standing in front of one another, barely a few inches between our faces. "What did you see? When I went boom?"

"I don't remember."

"Amnesia? That's awfully convenient." I test a hunch. "You yielded."

"I certainly did not!" he grits through his teeth.

The corners of my mouth quirk up. "Ah! So you do remember."

"No, but I know I would never have yielded to you."

"Cut the crap. You must remember. You said something about my eyes…"

The sneer he serves me could cut through glass. "Was it very romantic? You know what I think happened? I think you dreamed all this stuff up."

My pulse flies. "Let's make a deal. One time offer." The dark satisfaction that flicks in his eyes sends a shudder down my spine. "You tell me what happened and what you saw in my eyes, and I'll kneel for you. In front of everyone."

Never make a deal with a Fae, you'll end up on your knees.

He curses under his breath. "I can't make that deal."

He's not lying because there is absolutely no way he would have said no. He puffs his chest. "I propose another bet to settle the matter. Instead of beating me in Duel, you have to beat me in everything. You take the top spot this quarter, and we'll all leave you alone."

That's an enticing offer, but what's in it for him? "And if I don't?"

"You quit the Academy."

My breath stutters. I can't—He wants me out? Since when? I chew the offer and try to keep a straight face, but I'm shattered. Whatever game we were playing before is over. He hates me now.

"Okay. But if I beat you, you and your court have to stop bullying all mortals until graduation." I extend my hand and raise a brow, daring him to accept.

"Deal."

The steel in his handshake squeezes my palm to the point of pain, and I get the feeling I'll never touch him again.

The interlude has cost us a few precious minutes, and we arrive at S&S only to find the solid door closed.

Cole curses and slaps the wall with his opened palm. Deveraux closed the door, which means...

I grab my forehead and wince. "Neither of us is going to win if we don't pass S&S."

Cole turns on his heels. "We can work together and tear each other down, can't we?"

"Are you asking me?"

"Shape up, Sabrina. I wouldn't want my victory to be too easy."

I watch his back disappear around the corner and wonder what would have happened if Mr. Oz had let me beat up Flynn, or if I hadn't made that bet in the first place. Would Cole have mentioned his discovery of my peculiar parentage? If he knew what it meant, he probably would have outed me already.

Human or not, I'm still a mortal. I guess the difference is inconsequential to him.

I set up shop in one of the empty classrooms and turn the heat on my cauldron. I'm not going to let this morning go to waste, but Miss Deveraux's input would have been invaluable.

When I step outside the main building, about twenty minutes after my class ended, two things immediately feel wrong. One, a big, dead tree is standing out front where a luscious, proud Douglas Fir used to be. Second, my name is written in red across the grayish bark.

The Winslow Grinch who stole Christmas.

I inch toward the graffiti, my heart hammering.

What the—

As I'm about to graze the red paint, two branches shoot out and trap me in their strong grip. I shriek and twist around to free myself, but the hold only gets stronger. The branches scratch and tear at my clothes.

The tree holds my arms flat against my sides, spinning me around so I'm facing the main building. I can barely move. My fire sparks off in every direction and bounces off my enemy.

Flynn prowls up to me, his blond hair wafting in the wind, his chest puffed out.

He's got the same black shirt and red tie as Cole, and I notice other students are all wearing the same style. A crowd forms in front of my gnarly prison, and I fight against my restraints.

Flynn smirks. "We're all in mourning for our freedom."

"What are you babbling about?"

"I'm talking about the curfew we're stuck with, thanks to you." His eyes shine as they settle on the black satin of my bra.

I look down at my tainted, torn blouse. Tears sting my eyes, but I swallow them all. "You have an obsession with seeing me naked."

"Who would touch you now? You're a demon whore. How else would you be able to conjure infernal magic?"

"The only whore here is you, Flynn."

The jab rolls off him like water against the feathers of a vulture. "They should have expelled you. Your daddy must have sucked the President's dick himself for him to stick his neck out for you," he says.

He's so close, I could count his eyelashes.

The crowd thickens, and most of the students are wearing black and red.

Flynn points to his supporters. "See? I'm not the only one who thinks mortals should pack their bags. The first one we want out is you."

Cole is among them. The red tie from before jumps out at me now that I know what it stands for. Brie and Vivianne stand tall on each side of him. The cheery vampire's somber gaze is the most sobering of all.

Lydia shoots me a sad, regretful look, and heads out with Olson under the cackles of my detractors.

I swallow hard.

The battle lines have been drawn.

All we have left is war.

26

K.I.S.S.I.N.G

Being public enemy number one is no fun. Half the students are too scared to come within five feet of me, and the other half wants to punish me.

"Filthy mortal whore" gets tagged on all my desks, the red paint disappearing as soon as a teacher comes close. That's the downside of magic. Making someone's life hell is easy. Getting away with it is even easier.

The only ones who haven't completely disavowed me are Olson and the snake twins, though I'm still unsure if that's positive. Blane and Bailey treat me like a fellow criminal whose street cred is impressive enough to warrant a courteous nod when we cross paths in the halls.

All the girls whisper behind my back, and I actually miss high school where a witty comeback would have been enough to sweeten the acid in my throat.

Celeste Draco instituted the curfew as a "protective measure" on Christmas Eve. She knew exactly what she was doing. Sure, she wants to pass it off as an incentive for the immortals to watch out for us, but it's actually the exact opposite. The students are pissed, and I'm the ugly duckling amongst a litter of unwanted kittens.

Flynn was right. Everyone wants us gone so things can, quote, "get back to normal."

Lydia skips more and more classes. I know they're bullying her, maybe even more so than me, but she made it clear that she didn't want me around.

The library is the only semi-safe refuge. My notebooks cover every inch of the desk I used when I first came here, the one in the far back. I snarl at everyone who comes within five feet of me because I need to concentrate. I need to win. And if I can't earn these people's respect, I'll settle for their fear. Most of them are sheep wearing wolf masks.

Without Flynn, Cole, Jessa, or Brie, they're too cowardly to approach me.

When a silhouette casts a shadow over my papers, I raise my head and expect the worst, my tongue sharpened by all the rage simmering inside me.

Trent is standing in front of me, his hair pulled back, his face ashen.

"Funny. I haven't seen you all week." The hardness in my voice barely covers up my wretched mood.

He passes a hand over his face and slumps down on the chair across from mine. "I was in Europe. My grandfather died."

I glance up. "Oh." I'd assumed Trent and Melanie were avoiding me for fear of being guilty by association. "I'm sorry. I thought—" My fingers cramp around my pen, and I look down at my ink-tainted hands. A heavy lump sits in my throat. "Things have been rough here."

He moves to the empty seat next to me and cups my face. "Heard about that."

I welcome his kiss the way a drowning man clutches a buoy. It's fresh and sweet and stripped of any afterthought or scheme.

"What about the others? Isn't being seen with me a cardinal sin?"

"I don't give a fuck." He twines our fingers, brings my hand up to his mouth and kisses the back of it.

My shoulders sag. "I'm sorry about your grandfather."

He chucks out a low, painful laugh. "Don't be. He was mostly an ass."

"Then I'm sorry for thinking you abandoned me."

"You can make it up to me sometime." The bittersweet humor on his face pushes me into action.

I pack up my things quickly. "Come."

"Where?"

"Let's take a walk." I throw my jacket on without buttoning it and pull him along.

His fingers wrap around mine.

Once we're at a safe distance from the library, I stop abruptly and push Trent against a tree. He opens his mouth to speak, but I swallow his question with a searing kiss.

I tug on his tie—black, of course—and undo the first few buttons of his white shirt. The hard but cool planes of his chest tighten my gut, and I pull him along the path, eager for us to have some privacy.

The shadows thicken and offer a welcomed cover on our way to Summer Hall. My jacket comes off my shoulders as the temperature changes, and Trent's cool hands become more and more enticing. I'm fire. He's ice. We balance each other.

The stones near the limits of the garden push hard on my back as we kiss. Hunger blazes in his garnet eyes.

I'm about to tilt my head back and offer him my throat, giving him my trust in exchange for his loyalty, a fair trade by anyone's standards, when voices coax us out of the trance.

Trent and I dip below the cedar hedge.

"I'm just saying we could see more of each other," Mr. Oz says.

"Daniel..." The female voice belongs to Miss Eillis.

"Beth. We've been through this. I don't mind the limitations or sacrifices. I need you in my life."

I peer through the branches. Oz bends forward and captures her heart-shaped lips in a sensual kiss.

Miss Eillis stands on her tiptoes. She's tiny compared to the tall, rugged professor.

I stifle a giggle in my palm. I'm not the only one getting lucky tonight.

"Eillis and Oz sitting in a tree..." Trent chants below his breath.

I press my head into his shoulder. "I should go and study for my test tomorrow."

"Because of the deal you made with Cole," he grumbles unhappily.

My breathing hitches. I hardly think something like that would be public knowledge, but the arrogant prince has an even bigger mouth than I'd thought.

"Why did you let him under your skin?" Trent scolds.

I puff my chest. "I can beat him."

The vampire observes me for a minute like he's measuring my resolve before grinning. "You better. I don't want to visit my girlfriend in some second grade school."

I'm grateful for the humor in his voice, grateful that he doesn't try to baby me or talk me out of it. I'm going to beat Cole and already regret not asking him to leave the Academy if I win. I'll burn his pedestal down until he and his friends are barefoot in the mud and forced to see us as equals.

27

THE BAD GUY

A light knock resonates across my silent room. "Julia? I made some tea," Miss Eillis says before she enters my sanctuary.

I rub the fatigue away from my overworked face and grab the mug from her hand. "Thank you."

The mattress barely sags under her weight when she sits on Lydia's abandoned bed. Her knuckles grip the sides, and she tilts her head. "You're studying a lot these days."

My t-shirt hangs loose over my shoulders, and my hair is in knots. "I have to."

"I don't want to add to your workload, but your father asked me to tutor you."

The hot cinnamon tea warms my mouth, throat, and heart. "I know I missed a few key questions on that last test, but I think—"

"Not in Herbology. In infernal magic."

My mouth hangs open, and I consider Miss Eillis in a different light. Her long white hair is alive with magic, and her troubled stare always seems to mask how young she actually looks.

A thread sticks out of my duvet, and I play nervously with it. Does she know about me? About my mother? I doubt it, but you never know. "How do you know infernal magic?"

"That's not important. It's an incredible power that we possess, and I can help you harness it."

I meet her gaze head on. "What are you?"

The corners of her lips quirk up. I've been skirting around the issue since we met, and I detect a hint of satisfaction in her grin. "Do you have a theory?"

"No," I say honestly.

"Good. I wouldn't want to think my secrets are too easy to discover."

With that mysterious statement, she grins and opens her book. "First, I'm going to teach you how to channel infernal energy safely."

"But my dad said I shouldn't use these powers again."

A deep sigh heaves her chest. "But you will. Someday, the magic will come to you again, and I want you to know what to do with it. Don't worry, we won't break any rules to do it."

I nod.

"Close your eyes and focus on your breathing. Try to access the magic. Slowly."

Calling forth this magic isn't that much different than calling on my elemental powers. It's a path less traveled, but the door was smashed open by what I did the other day, and as soon as I allow myself to connect with that incredibly scary part of me, I find it again with ease.

Ants run along my arms. The energy beneath my skin feels like a lost limb that sparks to life again. It's mine.

A purple spark flies off my fingers, and matching veins run along my arms. I recoil from the intensity of it, but the more I try to turn it off, the more it spreads, clinging to my fingers. Long dark strands lick my hands until a tremor engulfs me from head to toe.

Miss Eillis twines our fingers, and the power melts into her. The wisps of purple smoke disappear into nothingness. "Good. That's very nice for a first try."

"It feels… untamable."

"It's wild, not untamable. We will practice again. Every day if we have to, until you learn to disengage by yourself."

160

She leaves with my empty cup, my mind full of questions.

* * *

After History of Magic, Trent escorts me out of the main building. His presence keeps most of my bullies at bay. Heat crawls on my cheeks when he twines our fingers for everyone to see.

Once outside, gravel drags under our boots, and we both reduce our pace at the sight before us. Across the main pathway, Lydia is arguing with Blane.

Blane wraps one arm around Lydia's shoulders and leads her toward the edge of the forest. She shakes her head vehemently, but the snake shifter pushes her along.

"I've got it." Trent hurries off and puts himself in their paths.

Blane shouts something that I can't hear, but Trent gives him one dark look, and the snake throws his arms in the air, releasing Lydia.

My ex-roommate hugs her chest.

Trent jogs back toward me. "I'll walk her to her dorm."

I squeeze his arm, touched by his concern. "Thank you."

"I'll come back."

"No need. I have to finish my Herbology essay. See you tomorrow."

They depart toward Lydia's new dorm, and I feign to head to Summer Hall but double back instead. Blane is still lurking on the outskirts of the main building, probably looking for another victim. The twin is tall and gangly, and his sunken cheeks aren't very intimidating. I can totally take him.

In long strides, I accost him right by the entrance and flatten him against the wall, my arm braced across his collarbone. "We need to talk."

The snake's sneer morphs into a mocking grimace. "Keep your hands off me, witch."

A trickle of flames singes his scruffy beard and drains the warmth from my voice until it's sharp, cold, and totally badass. "Afraid I'll blow your head off? You should be." I tilt my head slightly and inch closer to his face. "You're going to leave Lydia alone. No more pranks. No more threats."

He hisses in such a way that I half expect his tongue to come out and taste the air between us. "Or what? If you use forbidden magic again, you'll be expelled."

A smirk festers on my lips, the type of empty grin Flynn would serve me. "Only if they find out..."

I've got to turn my new reputation into an advantage, and I know from the sweat flowing from Blane's underarms that he'll keep his distance. Pride tickles all over. I puff out my chest and spread my shoulders to scare him off, and the serpent slithers away with his metaphorical tail tucked between his legs.

A genuine smile chases away the cold act.

Fuck. That was fun.

"Being bad is addictive, isn't it?" Cole's casual voice seeps through my clothes, skin, and cells like torrential rain.

I stiffen and slowly spin on my heels.

He leans casually against the brick wall and smirks like he hasn't missed a lick of what transpired.

"You want a turn?" I ask.

Danger flashes in his eyes. "Try me." He calls my bluff like he knows I won't dare touch him. The satisfaction written across his terribly beautiful face is unbearable. "Come. We have to do the S&S assignment."

"You're not the boss of me," I say, even though we do need to get cracking on the next spell on our list. This is as good a time as any, so I follow Cole's dark silhouette up the gravel path leading to the big stone gargoyle.

The library is quiet. A few students yawn among the stacks. Cole and I take my table, the one at the very back.

We both agreed on a truce not to flunk S&S, but these quiet moments at the library are killing me. Studying alongside Cole is a curse in itself.

The soft rustling of paper, the dim flicker of the torches, the spicy scent of his breath—everything fucks with my head.

It's calm. Intimate.

From the way he extends his legs underneath the table after being immobile for too long to the warmth of his knees bumping mine when he switches position, I can barely focus on the work. I keep waiting for an ambush or a cruel comment to break the serenity of our studying sessions only to be left even more rattled when nothing happens.

I scratch my neck, trying hard not to notice how the knot of his tie is loose enough to reveal the edge of his chest tattoo. The black ink contrasts with the white undershirt.

"Why do you want to stay here? When everyone is against you and your very life is in danger?" He asks without looking up.

"Because it's the best school."

"But to what end? You'll graduate, and then what? Maybe you have a few good years on the market, five at most. But you'll find a husband soon enough, marry, have kids. Even if you don't, you'll never be good enough to get into the Magisterium. These things take practice. Practice takes time, and time is precisely what you don't have." A casual shrug punctuates his litany.

Angry roaches scatter beneath my skin. "And why do you bother? You'll be given free passes and opportunities because of your last name, and you'll drown in alcohol and women until your narcissistic instincts command you to procreate."

A light flush colors Cole's cheeks, but he keeps a straight face. He returns the first book to his leather bag. "You'll never beat me, Sabrina."

"Why not?"

"I want it more," he says, like it's all a matter of will.

My knuckles clench over the edge of the table. "My whole future is at stake. I'm willing to do whatever it takes."

"And I'll do worse." It sounds more like a promise than a threat, his face serene.

The upbeat tone throws me for a loop, and I arch an eyebrow at him. "Why do you even care?"

A cloud passes over his eyes before he gets up, peels his jacket off the back of the chair, and whistles out.

When the main entrance closes behind him, I comb my hair back and blow out a deep breath through my mouth.

What a jerk. I can't let him rattle me like that.

After I get home, I unpack my bag. My fingers clasp the leather, and I rummage through the papers and books furiously.

My summary notes are missing. My entire work from the last three weeks—gone. Someone else must have stolen them while I was arguing with Cole, and now I can't study. The bastard set me up after all.

It takes me three full nights in the library to compensate for the stolen notes. It leaves me no time for anything else, but since I seem to have no one left besides Trent, I don't let it bother me too much.

The only thing that matters is beating Cole. After that, everything will fall into place. It has to.

28

DISTRACTIONS

"*Y*ou drive me crazy, Jules," Trent says.

I jab a finger in his side. "Watch your fangs, Darkwood."

One positive thing about being a pariah is that I get to be alone in my room, which is pretty convenient when I want to make out with my vampire boyfriend.

Trent is wrapped around me over my dark comforter. His jeans hang low on his hips, and his hair tickles my cheeks.

Cool lips linger on my neck. The playful tone of his voice barely covers the clear bloodlust on his face. "I swear you'd love it."

The scrape of his teeth scatters goosebumps across my chest. "I don't doubt that." The more I invite him over, the more I'm sure I want to try.

His fingers twitch over my hip. "Then what are we waiting for?"

"I don't know," I answer honestly. I shift to my elbows and grab my notebook on the nightstand.

Trent groans. "You know that book inside and out."

"I've had quite enough distraction for tonight. I have to ace this test tomorrow."

"You love my distractions," he says, hiking his hand up my side.

My whole body arches in response, and I almost toss the book to the ground but clench it instead. I can't spend the whole evening fooling around with him.

When I don't budge, he rolls off me and sags against the mattress. "I've taken this test already. If you let me bite you, I could show you a memory or two of it…"

I clamp my palm over his mouth. "Using your vampire memory-sharing voodoo to cheat on a test? Really?"

Vampires have the ability to merge a human's memory with their own during a bite. That's how they've managed to feed without being caught for so many centuries. They essentially replace the memory of the bite with something else, and the victim is none the wiser. As a supernatural being, I wouldn't be so easily manipulated. Trent could use this power to show me a moment from his past, but I don't want to cheat my way to victory.

He shrugs like his offer was no big deal, grabs his own homework and adjusts the pillow under his head. "We should go to the winter dance together." He casually flips a page of his book.

"Okay."

"Yes?" A big grin breaks across his face.

"Sure."

"I thought you'd fight me on this." He rolls me over and dives in for another kiss.

Studying be damned.

After a risqué make-out session, Trent talks me into a late night walk. The night is chilly but calm. The icy rain frosts over the tips of the pine trees at the edge of Summer Hall. The leaves of the tree in the middle of the garden have orange and yellow edges.

Like Miss Eillis predicted, winter is coming.

I run my fingers through the cedar hedge, and the stiff needles prickle my skin.

Trent points to the sky. "Full moon."

The bright, imperial silver disk shines above our heads, and the stars shy away from its light. A blue halo is visible around it, which means it's a perfect night to cast a powerful spell.

As Trent kisses me goodnight, a rustling in the trees sets my teeth on edge.

A hunched form staggers out of the forest, and I squint. A sense of dread blooms in my chest. A girl walks aimlessly among the tall pines. The red and white uniform barely sticks to her bloody skin.

My heart plunges past my feet before my brain truly grasps what's happening. "Oh my Gods, Lydia!" I break into a run. My lungs burn, my entire body shaking.

Blood flows down her knees, and she grips my hands to steady herself upright. "Jules?" Hooded eyes seem to look past me without seeing me.

"What happened? Tell me!" I scream, unable to rein the panic in.

She grips my arm, her fingers digging into my flesh. "You need to leave. You need to leave before it kills us all." Her high-pitched, feminine voice sounds like tiny diamonds scattered across glass.

She slumps down, and Trent is there in time to stop her head from hitting the ground.

I gape, frozen, and cling to her body until Miss Eillis and Mr. Oz come running. Mr. Oz checks Lydia's vitals and her injuries.

Bent over the worst of the cuts, a nasty slash on her thigh, I barely notice the worry on their faces before Miss Eillis touches my shoulder. "Julia."

"We need to find who did this," I croak.

Mr. Oz wipes the blood off his hands on the front of his pants. "I'll alert the doctor that we're coming and report the incident. Did you see anything?"

I shake my head.

Miss Eillis sinks her fingers in the bed of moss. The ground vibrates under her touch as she molds the earth beneath my friend to make a stretcher. That's advanced elemental magic, and I stand in awe. The molecules of dirt reassemble, and four branches act as handles at the corners.

I move to grab one, but Mr. Oz blocks my way gently with his hand.

"You shouldn't be here when the Magisterium agents come," he says.

"I found her. They might have questions."

He angles me to him. "Listen closely, Julia. You said yourself you have no idea what happened. Whatever you saw the other day in the woods, it was from the underworld."

My eyes widen.

Miss Eillis pats my shoulder. "People are afraid of what they do not understand. Infernal magic is one of them. Demons are another. They also don't believe in coincidences. These attacks started the week that you arrived, and now your roommate is involved. They're going to try to pin this on you."

I shake my head. "Lydia and I are friends."

"They'll say she asked you not to speak to her anymore. That you were angry," Oz says.

My head is spinning.

Trent squeezes my hand. "Go inside, Jules. I'll tell them I found her myself."

I obey and watch from the back bay window as they haul Lydia out on the magic stretcher.

The Magisterium agents install a magic barrier around the scene, most of them heading off into the woods. A small crowd forms by the edge of the garden, and a few students lurk for a whiff of gossip.

When two dark spots detach from the mass and head toward the porch, I back away from the window and pace the kitchen. Will Trent get into trouble for lying? Will the lie make my part in this more suspicious?

I should have stayed out there.

This was a mistake.

A loud knock startles me, my heart beating furiously.

"Jules?"

It's Olson.

With a frown, I crack open the front door.

Olson is standing on the terrace, dark circles under his eyes. Jeremy is with him. The burly werewolf's fists shake at his sides.

168

I catch them up on the situation.

"We need to sneak into those woods," Jeremy growls.

"We can't go now," Olson negotiates. "We need to catch whoever did this and get revenge. Show we're not going to be chased out of school by some lunatic."

My mouth is dry, but the panic from before has mostly lifted. "What are you thinking?"

"It's got to be one of them. The Fae have been at the head of the anti-mortal movement since the beginning. Your boy Cole has got to be the head of the snake."

I pinch Olson's arm hard. "He's not my boy."

The warlock winks and whispers, "We need to trick him into showing his cards. Make him mad enough to be reckless. Do you really think you can win your bet?"

"Absolutely, but I'm not going to stoop as low as they are. I want to win in my own right." Whatever Olson is saying, I have trouble imagining Cole attacking Lydia or Holly like that in cold blood.

The blue-haired warlock punches the air in front of him. "Playing fair is going to get you expelled, and Cole and his minions will graduate with honors while you take up some bullshit job as some politician's assistant."

I open my mouth in protest.

He wraps an arm around me and kicks off his shoes. "Hear me out, Jules. I've got your back."

29

SCANDALOUS

*T*hey should have renamed the hide and seek game to fuck over Jules night.

Flynn is a hider this time around but prowls up and down the starting line, his cat eyes fixed on me. It's clear from the moment the start horn blazes that the seekers are gunning for me first.

I run into the trickiest part of the forest where the trees are closely knit together, toward the steep rock wall that leads to the top of the falls. I've prepared the ingredients for a spider climb spell.

The night is foggy and bleak, and a few patches of ice make the terrain treacherous.

I steal a glance over my shoulders, half-expecting everyone to be on my tail, but only one pair of quickened footsteps thuds behind me.

As soon as I reach the rock, Flynn is on me.

He grabs a fist of my hair before I have a chance to move and yanks my head back. "Why did you bother? We were never going to let you win." The satisfied smirk on his face makes my skin crawl.

He imprisons me in a bear hug and drags me out into the open. I twist and wrestle in his hold, trying to squirm free, but the more I wiggle, the tighter he squeezes me against his chest. The warmth of his body is devious and alluring compared to the cold night air.

I finally relax and aim a fist at his side.

Quick as a snake, he blocks my blow and hauls me over his shoulder. My upper body hangs in midair, my stomach braced against the muscles of his shoulder blades. He feels like Cole, like an unmovable rock wall splitting me in two. His coat is thick enough that I don't have access to his skin, but I still press both my palms over his back and push my fire through.

Flynn doesn't seem bothered by the heat, his steps quick and self-assured until the flames pierce through the leather.

As I glimpse an inch of his skin, a large hand squeezes my ass.

My breath catches. A sickening warmth sparks from his hands to the tips of my fingers and toes. I growl a curse of profanity before being tossed onto a cold bed of moss.

A hateful circle closes around me. Brie. Vivianne. Melanie. Jessa. Cole.

"Here she is," Flynn announces proudly.

Brie touches my wrist, and the number 1 appears in neon red calligraphy. "It's done."

I jump to my feet, my head still spinning from the fall.

"Now, let's find her friends," Vi says.

The other seekers are all on board to spare Flynn and hunt us. Just like Olson had predicted.

Brie braces her fist on her hip. "We have to concentrate on her sister."

Melanie shakes her head. "She's never found. She shows up in time not to be a seeker, but nobody knows where that witch hides."

Cole moves to the center of the evil huddle. "Let's go. We need to find the other mortals."

Now that I've officially lost, they all seem to be ignoring me. All but Flynn. A wicked smile spreads over his mouth as he checks the hole I made in his coat.

"One of them is a seeker," Brie clarifies, heading off with Melanie. "He managed to get away, so be careful."

Cole leans towards Jessa and whispers, "Find Darkwood. We're sending a message. Anyone who's with them is against us."

They fan out in search of the others, but Flynn doesn't budge.

Cole stops at the edge of the trees. "Are you coming?"

"In a minute," Flynn answers. He looks me up and down in such a way that I can't help but check myself to see if anything is wrong with my clothing, but no.

I wrap my arms around my frame and tap my foot on the icy ground. "You got me. Congratulations. Can I go now?"

"The night is just beginning." He snaps his fingers, and the tree behind me wraps its branches around my collarbone.

The hug is not as vicious as it was the other day. "What are you? The Tree whisperer?"

My sass is met with silence. The contemplative gaze unnerves me more than the hatred from before.

The dark ninja outfit hugs his broad frame and makes him practically invisible in the thick darkness. The beanie covering his blond locks is the same as the one he was wearing the morning after the divination field trip, and he tears it off his head. "You think you're on our level."

"Not at all. I think I'm better." I enunciate the words to piss him off and check the branches holding my wrists. The wood is dry and would catch on fire quickly.

Flynn wags his index finger from side to side. "You don't want to set fire to the forest. That would get you expelled faster than any trick I have up my sleeve." He closes the distance between us. The grimace on his face melts into something foreign.

The hairs at the back of my neck rise to attention, and I try to push the branches. My wrists scream at the abuse, but the wood holds strong. "Stay back, or you'll burn first."

His fingers poke the hollow of my neck and drag downward. "Kneel for me, and I'll let you go." The way he says the words is both cajoling and hopeful.

The Fae glamor plays hide-and-seek with his sharp cheekbones, the beauty of him enhanced by the magic in his veins. He's pushing every ounce of it my way, and desire spikes in my blood.

"Come on, do it for me."

My throat bobs.

A dark glint dances in his all-consuming stare. He's hoping I'll break for him. Like whoever gets me to kneel in front of them first will be crowned king.

The compulsion is strong, but tonight, I am stronger. The salt water I gulped down right before the horn blasted is still rumbling in my belly.

When his hand closes around my neck, I no longer feel like this is a game. Flynn would choke the life out of me without question, and my breath stutters.

A hard hand tests my pulse point, and the heat of his rash breaths scalds my cheeks.

I press my head against the bark to put as much distance between our faces as I can. When his fingers grow soft around my throat, I stop breathing altogether.

He's close enough for me to see the silver ring around his irises, and the proximity chokes me better than the hand at my neck. The tip of his nose rubs my cheek, the soft caress almost obscene.

I hold his gaze. If I look away, he'll close the gap between us and serve me a kiss that will ruin me.

We stay like that for a while, frozen in defiance, neither of us willing to break the spell first.

Giggles echo in the night, and Flynn doubles back. He tears at his hair and shakes his hands out.

Jessa skips closer and closer. Allie flinches under her grip.

Joy engulfs me at the sight, but I school my features into a frown.

"Got her sister." Jessa hands her over to Flynn with a deviant grin.

Cole is behind her, and the two male Fae grab a hold of Allie and drag her to the tree next to me.

The smile on my sister's face is completely unnatural. She tilts her head back and laughs.

The boys pause.

With a slight shimmer, Allie's tight face melts into Olson's. The warlock grins from ear to ear. Flynn and Cole yank their hands away, but it's too late. They all touched him. Our seeker.

If my hands weren't tied up, I would applaud.

The Fae stare in horror at the red numbers written inside their palms. Jessa yelps and checks her skin, too.

I burst out laughing. "Looks like I won't be the only one on dish duty this month."

Flynn's hand closes around Olson's throat. "You're dead, Lewis."

Olson snorts. "You're found, Verinos. Might as well not humiliate yourself further."

The branches secure my friend into a similar prison as my own as Flynn spits to the ground. "I heard there's a beast roaming these woods. With some luck, we'll find you both in pieces tomorrow morning."

With a growl that's more animal than man, Cole follows his friend down the trail. His sinister gaze flicks over to me for one short second.

His gaze is so drastically different from what it used to be. Before, it'd be calculating, but heated—playful even. Now, it's all thorns and resentment. The dark pits betray nothing but utter contempt. Gone is the soft edge of his touch, gone is the teasing sound of his voice. There is nothing but cold marble and a deserted emptiness where the sparks between us used to flicker.

I miss it sometimes, though I'd never admit it to anyone. Cole might have wanted me before, but now he wants me gone. Dead. Buried. I'm living proof that he's not invincible, and he'll always hate me for it.

All for the best. I'm a Winslow. He's a Fae prince. We're bound to kill each other at some point.

They leave us chained to the trees. A cold wind rushes along my neck, but I can barely feel it. "Your plan worked," I say to Olson.

"I told you it would. You just had to distract them long enough."

We mime a high five from our precarious positions.

Turning into someone else is an incredibly advanced spell. No way Olson was able to cast that on his own.

"Who helped you?" I ask.

He presses his index finger to his mouth. "That's a secret."

"Is Lydia okay?"

"She's regained consciousness, but I heard she doesn't remember a thing."

I bite my bottom lip hard enough to taste iron on my tongue.

Olson winks, his chest puffed out like he's the king of the jungle. "Allie is going to come in around fifteen minutes. And then we can plan our next attack."

"Attack?" I raise a brow.

He laughs it off. "You know what I mean."

I do. It's about serving the immortals their just desserts, with whipped cream and humiliation on top. The way things keep escalating, we might even set the whole thing on fire and make a crème brûlée.

30

THE FIRST BITE

*T*he winter dance is a barely-veiled excuse for students and staff to dress like movie stars and drink the night away. There's a similar tradition in every school on Earth, and probably beyond, where everyone can gather, pretend they all like each other, and pat themselves on the back for being the best. I won't reward their dark, empty souls by skipping it.

My purple dress has a fluffy skirt that hides the shorts I'm wearing underneath. It's got a conservative neckline but dips really low down my spine, the v-shaped silk finishing right above said shorts. I've got a few spells hidden in a holster around my thigh in case Flynn, Cole, or anyone else tries to screw me over.

This dance is a very high-profile event. Nothing spells trouble like the promise of a public humiliation. I've seen enough Carrie remakes.

Trent shows up at Summer Hall five minute early, and I stagger when I see him. He's never looked like the son of Theodore Darkwood, billionaire, philanthropist, and cutthroat politician. Until now.

His tux is perfectly tailored to highlight his muscled frame, and the dark blue shade makes his skin look shiny instead of pale. His long hair is loose but styled away from his face. The volume and thickness of his brown mane prevents the hairstyle from looking flat or oily.

The messy locks contrast nicely with his clean-cut black undershirt and tie.

"Wow," he says as I throw on a long black jacket. "You look every bit the smart, sexy temptress that you are."

"You look every bit the billionaire playboy you want to be."

He takes my hand and leads me away.

The dining hall's been glamored to look like a ballroom. An enchantment transformed the ceiling into a clear starry sky, and diamond chandeliers twinkle in mid-air above our heads. The tables are gone, replaced by a live band playing supernatural radio sensations.

Trent rests a hand against my neck, and his thumb grazes my hairline. "I'll get us a drink."

Everyone whispers at our arrival. I'm an outcast, but Trent is more influential than I gave him credit for. A few students offer me a small smile.

Most students have ditched the black and red anti-mortal colors for the occasion, but Flynn didn't.

He skips over to me and showcases the sleeves of his jacket. "Do you like it? I had it specially made." The motif spells out "Julia Winslow should be expelled" in small, black script over a white background. His blond hair is slicked back for the occasion, enforcing the villainous look.

He prowls in a circle around me. "Cat got your tongue?"

I eye him up and down. "Went to all this trouble for me? Aw! I know you're obsessed with me, and I do appreciate the reliability of your efforts."

One corner of his mouth curls up before he steps into my personal space. "Dance with me."

I skip around him. "Over my dead body."

"Come on. I'm here with Melanie. You're with Trent. This is practically a double date."

The way he wets his lips while looking at my cleavage makes my heart squirm.

"Get lost, Verinos." Trent hands me a flute of champagne.

I down it in one gulp and take his outstretched hand.

Flynn glowers, but returns to Mel. She shoots me a nasty look over her red wine, and I spin around to erase her sullen pout from my vision.

Miss Eillis is radiant in a green gown that leaves her stomach bare, her long white hair braided into an intricate fishtail with teal and emerald highlights. Oz beams next to her, his arm wrapped around her waist.

Allie is there, looking drop-dead-gorgeous in a blue sleeveless sequined dress. She's hanging out with Olson and the other mortals and waves us over.

"Looking good, sis," she says, kissing me on the cheek.

"You, too."

Jeremy arrives with Lydia in tow. My ex-roommate is wearing a V-neck green dress and glittering heels. Gone is the mayhem and the blood.

"Hey," she says quietly, holding her clutch to her chest.

"Hey," I answer. "Are you okay?"

"I've been better, but I convinced my parents to let me stay." She offers me a smile. That's a start.

"No date?" Jeremy asks my sister.

Allie rolls her eyes. "One day you'll have to stop chasing me, wolf. Besides, it's a dick move to sniff around me when you're here with Lydia." She drops her flute on a table and leaves the room.

I almost want to punch Jeremy for driving her away.

The rest of us chat and try the specialty chocolates. The flavor I pick is marked as "salted caramel surprise" and starts out as a regular piece of chocolate before slowly fizzing into an explosion of bubbles. They roll pleasantly on my tongue and tickle all the way down my throat.

I grin and plop another one in my mouth.

Trent steals a taste with a kiss. "Yum. If you'll excuse me for a minute, I'll be right back."

Lydia hums after biting down on a "singing dulce de leche."

Maybe we can be friends again. As much as I'd love to sweep this whole nonsense under the rug, I'm still raw about it. Strict parents or not, she stood there while I was tied to a tree and did nothing to stop it.

Jeremy whisks her away to the dance floor, and I'm left alone with the tray of delicacies before Melanie corners me.

The train of her dress rattles behind her like a snake's tail. "You're hurting him. You see that, right? It's bad enough that he's into you, but he's alienating everyone else trying to defend you. He'll go to war for you. That's who he is. You should do the right thing and cut him loose."

I swallow the last of the "spicy hot fudge" and press a napkin to my lips. "Why would I turn away the only immortal who's decent enough to talk to me?"

She scowls. "Because you don't love him. You're just curious about the whole vampire thing. It's me, girl. We both know who you're really into."

I roll my shoulders back and meet her suspicious gaze without an ounce of shame. I won't take crap from a girl who's fucking Flynn willingly. "I have no idea what you mean."

"Save your badass savior crap for your own kind. I see you. Your little crusade is not about making things better for mortals. It's about you and your war against the Fae. Do us all a favor and fuck one already."

She scampers off as Trent returns.

"What did she want?" he asks.

"Nothing," I lie.

We laugh, kiss, and drink the night away until more and more people filter out.

A lovely rendition of an old love ballad blasts through the speakers, and Trent drags me to the dance floor and holds me close. The way his body molds to mine is intoxicating.

I rest my head on his shoulder.

His hands skim my ass before settling in a safe spot at my lower back. "Want to go somewhere more private?"

My mouth is dry, and I search for an answer in the crowd.

Melanie and Flynn are immediately on our right. Trent's twin shoots a murderous glare my way.

Lydia is dancing with Jeremy on the side. The wolf's tie hangs around his neck, undone.

Cole and Jessa are dancing, too, barely a few feet away. The prince's large shoulders are stiff underneath his black jacket, and his long fingers dig into the silk of his partner's dress.

So far, I'd been doing a stellar job of ignoring his existence.

I drag my gaze from Cole's sleeve up to his freshly shaved jaw to the rings on top of his ear. The disheveled curls give him a wild look. Jessa is the perfect trophy wife, her blue hair styled into a glamorous bun, her white dress revealing her every curve. A shine reverberates off them as though a special spotlight illuminates their path.

My lids flutter, erasing their presence.

Trent's cool thumb traces the slope of my neck. "Are you game?" he asks again, his voice heavy with promises.

I open my mouth to answer, but the words die on my lips. I'm staring right into Cole's amber gaze. The rich shade turns into liquid gold, his eyes narrowing slightly.

My throat is too tight for air to flow into my lungs. "I have to go to the bathroom. I'll meet you outside." I kiss Trent for good measure before heading toward the back.

My heels clack against the polished hardwood.

Over the squeaky-clean sinks, I let the cold water run down my wrists. I don't have to go out there and let Trent bite me. I don't have to lose my virginity, in any sense of the word. I can just tell him I'm tired.

Only...I'm not tired. He stuck his neck out for me when nobody else would, and I get all the right feels when we kiss.

I don't know why I'm hesitating. Is it an unconscious fear of being bitten? Is it the sex? I feel like I'm holding out for something, but the thought is so ludicrous that I won't allow my brain to form it.

My breaths are steady when I finally meet my gaze in the mirror. I'm going to march out there and let that sexy vampire bite me. We'll see where that leads.

A burst of icy wind breezes between my bare legs as I exit the dining hall, and a white puff of air rises into the darkness. It's at least ten degrees colder than when we arrived. I tighten my jacket around my frame. There's only one set of footsteps in the thin blanket of snow, and it's heading toward the cliff, so I follow the trail.

I search for Trent beyond the veil of thick, silent snowflakes, but my eyes settle on a very different, disturbingly familiar pair of shoulders.

Cole stands in the cold, looking out at the sea, his hands shoved in his pockets. His black tuxedo blurs with the shadowy sky at his back, and the polished shoes clash against the white snow.

We're only a few feet apart, and I stop abruptly, my legs like lead below me. My gaze searches the night, and I almost expect his friends to pop out from the sides and beat me up, but we're alone.

The look he gives me is one of fury and rancor, as though he hates me so much it interrupted his evening, hates me enough to shove me over that cliff. He doesn't say a word and leaps forward so fast I can't even process the movement.

Utter shock prevents me from fleeing or attacking.

With the darkest frown twisting his face, Cole grips the sides of my head and crushes his lips to mine.

One kiss.

No preamble. No restraint.

Just lips and tongues and desire wrapped into one twisted confession.

My hands snake around his forearms, and my nails dig into the expensive fabric of his jacket to push him away, but I open my mouth instead. The rush of adrenaline bashes my fears to fucking smithereens.

The soft swipes are sweeter than Fae fruit, but the harsh hand at the back of my head sings a very different tune. My palms end up flush against his chest and slip below the satin lapels of his tuxedo, searching for his heat. A hint of absinthe lingers on his breath. His spicy, natural scent plays with the strings in my belly.

He draws back and stares deep into my eyes with pride before angling my face for a deeper taste. A strong, willful arm snakes around my waist and crushes me to him. The outline of his torso sets my nerves ablaze, my breasts pushed hard against him.

Rage and fury taint every brush. His lips curse me in a language that's both thrilling and foreign, his tongue claiming my mouth with a dark possessiveness that scares me to my core. A white-hot fire trails from my mouth to my navel. The desperate clutch of his hands at my back howls for my complete and total submission.

The steel grasp doesn't relent, and I find myself tugging on his dark curls, pulling him closer, not away.

He growls and nips my bottom lip.

I rake my nails across his neck.

We spur each other on until we're out of breath, his tux wrinkled, my jacket half-torn from my shoulders.

It's rough and messy and fucking unbelievable.

So impossible, so wrong, so forbidden.

But oh-so-good.

My mind rears its head in the chaos. We vowed to tear each other down. Why am I still kissing him?

Why did he kiss me in the first place?

You know why, that little voice in my head chants.

Snowflakes pepper his long eyelashes. "Don't let him be your first."

A dizzying need to agree spirals in my bones. I want to close my eyes, lean into Cole's arms and forget why I can't. Instead, I push him and growl, "Excuse me?"

His rage doubles. My neck falls victim to his assaults as he bites the tender flesh of my pulse point. My lids flutter.

"Jules?" Trent's voice booms from the way I came, beyond the wall of snow, beyond the insanity of this moment.

I blink, and I'm standing alone on the cliff. A drizzling rain beats against my heated cheeks. There's no snow, no trails of footsteps to give me away. It was all a spell, a ruse to get me alone.

"Jules?"

"I'm here," I call out, my voice trembling.

Trent catches up to me and eyes me up and down. "You okay?"

I tighten my jacket around my body and nod.

"What's that?" He gathers a drop of blood from my neck with his thumb.

My breath stutters. "I must have nicked myself with something."

Something like my Archnemesis' teeth.

Trent puts his thumb in his mouth and hums. His eyes close for a split second. "You taste…"

He bends down to kiss me, but I clasp his shoulders. "Wait."

He freezes and sniffs the air, his eyes searching for something. "What's wrong?"

Would he taste Cole on my guilty tongue? "Nothing, I—" Half of me wants to run for cover. The other half wants to make Trent my first everything right here right now. My head spins from the possibility. "I'm not ready."

A flash of hurt passes in Trent's ruby eyes. "I see."

"It's not about you."

"I know. I'm not—It's fine that you're not ready. If that's really the reason. Tell me, Jules, is that really the reason?"

"Yes. What else would it be?"

A sad smile grazes his lips, and he throws one arm around me. "Come on, Winslow. I'll walk you home."

And damn if I'm not the most confused, aroused, and completely screwed witch on campus.

31

WICKED GAMES

his year's Beach Games will be held in Faerie. For security reasons, mortals aren't allowed.

Olson tears the purple flier from the door of the auditorium and crumples it angrily. "It's bullshit. They're segregating us to make a point."

The Beach Games are an Academy tradition. It's all everyone has been talking about for the last few days. Students get to practice spells and compete in challenges. This last-minute change to the rules is probably Celeste's doing, and I tug on my bikini strap angrily. She made us get ready only to leave us in the dust. Figures.

Allie smiles mischievously. "Let's go anyway."

"What? How?" I ask, surprised at the sureness in her tone.

She wiggles her brows. "We know someone who might be willing to help. I've heard Oz could get us into Faerie."

Lydia shifts from foot to foot. "I really don't think…"

Olson punches his palm. "Let's do it. Let's show them we won't take their crap without fighting back."

When we get to Winter Hall, Mr. Brady is deep in conversation with Mr. Oz.

The two teachers together are a sight to see. Their weekend

clothes and relaxed behavior give me hope that our pleas will be heard.

Allie explains our situation to them both.

"I don't know, guys. It's a new rule, but a rule nonetheless," Mr. Brady says, rubbing his jaw.

Oz pats his back. "Come on, Jack. It sounds pretty harmless with the right precautions. I used to love these parties when I was a student. I bet the Fae just left the mortals out of it to spite them." He fumbles in his desk. "Take salt with you and wear these." He hands us charms made to look like necklaces.

We each wrap the cherry wood jewelry around our necks.

Oz wheels a large rectangular-shaped object in from the back. It's covered with a black velvet sheet, and my heart hammers as he unveils it.

The gold frame of the mirror shimmers under the candlelight. The glass reflects a version of us that's so appealing and beautiful that I don't dare look directly at my face.

Me. As a Fae. What a scary visual.

"A Faerie portal," Olson gasps.

I arch a brow. According to Dad, only a few select sorcerers are allowed to keep one.

Oz smiles. "It'll take you where you need to go. As long as you're wearing the necklaces, you'll be safe. Just come back with the others. They might not have agreed to take you there, but they won't be able to prevent your return." His gaze latches on to mine. "And be safe."

I nod and barrel through the glass first.

Cold bites into my flesh as Fae magic sinks deep into my pores. A thin film of ice forms on my skin, and before I know it, I'm in Faerie.

The otherworldly landscape is blinding in its treacherous beauty. Colors fill the space and textures come to life in a way that my brain takes a minute to process. Red is bloody, pink is sweet, blue is poignant. The tree's bark comes alive with wrinkles that seem to dance to an unheard tune. Purple and gold leaves waft in the wind and fill me with a sense of wonder I immediately squash down.

My face can't betray me.

This is enemy territory, and I'm here to make a point, not fangirl over the view.

Olson is right behind me. Allie follows.

Light reverberates off the white sand of the pristine beach. I squint and hold a hand over my forehead, letting my pupils adjust. When I spot Cole and Flynn in their bathing suits, I swallow hard and force my eyes not to stray past their chins.

This is going to be a very hot day.

The blonde Fae's gaze slides over us before he jumps off the rock he's sitting on, his carefree smile slapped off his face by the sight of us. He barrels closer and points the end of his white sunglasses at me. "You guys aren't allowed here."

Goosebumps tighten my skin. Sweat sticks to my palms as Cole twists around to look at me. The taste of his kiss fizzes over my lips, a bittersweet memory dipped in powdered sugar and venom. I walk in front of the others up the sandy path and concentrate on Flynn. "It's Faerie, not your backyard. You don't hold claim to a whole realm."

Flynn brings a hand to his chest. "Me? No. But we have a prince with us. Technically, his father owns all of Faerie."

I dig my heels in the sand and swat his comment away with the back of my hand. "Fine. Banish us back to the Academy if you're that scared that we're going to win your silly little game."

Cole chucks out a dark laugh, but he doesn't move from his spot. Jessa is sprawled on his lap, and his cold eyes don't spare me more than a glance.

It makes me doubt that Saturday night was real.

"We could beat your lot with our eyes closed," Flynn seethes.

I smile ear-to-ear. "Then prove it."

Flynn opens his mouth and meets Cole's gaze. After a second, he nods and steps out of our way. "Okay. Welcome to the Fae beach games, mortals. May the odds be ever in your favor."

I strip off my shirt.

Trent runs up to us. "I'll play with you." His hand is already on my arm, his gaze devouring the golden tan I got during Christmas break.

I squeeze his hand but shake my head. "Not today. Today, this is my team." I look back to my people. Allie. Olson. Lydia.

We can do it.

The volleyball tournament is first. Only magic is allowed to touch the ball, and Allie represents us proudly. Lydia wins the divination challenge to immortal boos but ear-numbing claps and encouraging shouts from us. Olson is neck to neck with Flynn at the climbing wall.

I hold back, waiting for Cole to take part in the celebrations. I want to give him a taste of how it feels to lose to me.

Melanie jumps on an empty bench and starts explaining the rules of the water treasure hunt. "Who's up for a real challenge? Whoever can find the mythic Dark Falls crown first will be king of the games."

"Or queen," Brie says quickly. She links her arm in Melanie's.

"A crown. Sounds like my cue to act," Cole says.

"We have Brie for the supernaturals, Cole for the Fae, anyone else?" Melanie arches a brow.

Dusting off my butt, I stand up.

"Don't, Jules. Something bad is going to happen, I can feel it," Lydia calls out.

I march ahead, and my skin tingles. I'm ignoring a direct warning from a seer, but I can't lay down and let these immortal assholes walk all over me. "Don't worry, guys, I won't let them win.

32

A MERMAID'S KISS

*T*he water is so dark; I'm blind. I can't believe I agreed to this. I push my way through slimy seaweed, knowing that I only have a few minutes. Magic or no magic, breathing under water requires serious concentration, and a headache is already forming between my eyes.

My lungs ache as I descend deeper and deeper into the abyss. Deep Fae water is treacherous, but I push through the stinging claustrophobia. The suffocating liquid bites my skin, and fear races behind my useless eyes.

The crown is at the bottom of the Fae sea. It emits a tiny magical signature that every supernatural can feel in their bones, but following it requires a lot of instinct. My witchy nature needs to be completely attuned to the elements despite the hostile surroundings.

A deep breath of salty water enters my nose. My enchanted lungs begrudgingly assimilate the oxygen, and I hum to drown out the silence until I feel it. The tiniest pull. As soon as I've got a good hold on the magic beacon, I dash in its direction.

Cold water swirls around me and bites into my flesh.

I bump into a rock and pat down my forehead.

It moves and paws at my arm.

Not a rock, then.

Not a rock skims my shoulders until it reaches my hair.

My hand finds silky skin. The hard planes of a man's chest heave underneath my fingers. My body recognizes what it craves, and my insides curl.

Nose against nose. Wet curls in my grip.

A hot, arrogant mouth meets my sullen pout and parts my lips.

We're quite literally hanging on this moment, our limbs floating in a thick, murky sea that makes us both blind and careless. I revel in the taste of this sinister indulgence as my mind screams at the self-betrayal.

My skin itches, and flames lick my insides. I snap my eyes open. A trail of light slowly rises from my chest and chases away the protective cover of darkness.

Cole freezes, and his eyes reflect the fiery hues.

The crown is ten feet below us, directly beneath our feet.

I make the first move, using my arms to propel me deeper, and shift myself upside down.

Cole grips my ankle and yanks me up. I stretch my fingers and graze the top of the jeweled mermaid crown.

Then, as though someone flipped a switch off, my lungs explode into a torrent of pain. I choke on an icy mouthful of Faerie water. My whole body cramps in panic. A hard arm closes around my waist. Cole pulls me away from the treasure and closer to the surface, and we both erupt over the water in a fit of coughs. I spit out water and heave until the taste of drowning is chased off my tongue.

We're probably miles from the start point. I stagger up a flat rock. It's night here in this pocket of Faerie reality. The thin moon rays filter through the dark rumbles of the streams that tumble down into the silvery sea.

"You bastard. I almost had it." Water drips down my back, my breathing ragged.

Cole wipes his dark hair away from his forehead and chases after me. "Did you fuck him?"

It takes me a moment to catch up. We're back to our conversation from the other night. "How dare you—"

His lips quirk up like he's reading the truth on my face. In a blur, he leans in and crushes his mouth to mine again.

This time, I keep my wits and shove him off. The slippery rocks under our feet offer questionable footing, so I jump to the grassy bank. "Fuck off."

The smile that was blooming on his lips turns into a lopsided scowl. "You didn't seem so angry with me in the water."

I throw my hands in the air. "Before you tried to drown me!"

His palm slices the space between us. "I saved you! Look, I'm not jumping for joy about it, but you've got to admit there's something between us."

A slippery shallow full of seaweed almost causes me to fall face-first into the water. "We hate each other. That's what's between us."

"Call it whatever you want. It's something." He slithers off the rocks, too. The steep cliff at my back offers no escape. "My friends would disown me for this. Hell, my mother would banish me to Faerie."

"Wow, listing all the people that think me inferior to you is really helping your cause."

His fist curls and opens again. "I hate *it*. Not *you*. This...whatever. It's annoying as fuck." The words are so quiet I barely hear them.

He's close now, close enough that I can see the droplets of water sticking to his eyelashes. The fabric of my swimsuit fails to hide my taut nipples. He leans in again, but I sink my fingers into his shoulder. This can't happen. Not here. Not anywhere.

A hot shudder quakes my body when his thumb traces my bottom lip, making me rethink that assessment.

"You're trying to run me out of school," I breathe.

"I'll make you a deal, Fire Girl. You kiss me again and hate it, and I'll leave you alone for the rest of your life. No more pranks. No more stolen notes. No more trouble."

I meet his gaze and relish the obvious desire in it. "One kiss."

"By the Dark Gods, I swear it."

His lips are confident and ravenous.

My elbow bumps the rock wall, and my nails dig into his chest. The hard grooves of his stomach contract underneath my fingertips, and I trace his tattoos.

The more I get, the needier I become. Each kiss is only a preamble to the one that comes next, the urgency increasing. The boldness of his hands against my sides steal my breath and what's left of my sanity. Cole is a drug. A beautiful, seductive, destructive drug.

When his hands slide below the fabric of my bikini bottoms, the tender skin of my hips aches for his touch to creep lower. I tear my mouth away. "It was odious." My heart beats furiously in my throat at the falsehood.

A dark chuckle vibrates across my neck. "Liar, liar, witch on fire."

He traces the swirly flames licking the hollow of my neck down to the space between my breasts with a proud, vile grin.

I lost. I made a deal with a Fae and lost.

My fists curl, my stupid heart in knots. A dark, heavy shadow rattles inside me, eclipsing the self-loathing.

Standing on my tiptoes, I press my lips back into Cole's...and bite him.

A steely, spicy hint of Fae blood explodes across my tongue.

Hand hard behind my head, he presses me to him. He did that the first time, crushing me to his mouth like he owns me. It drives me wild.

I shove him off. "Swear to me that you're not Allie's secret boyfriend. Swear that nothing happened between you two on Halloween?" I watch and listen intently not to be fooled by a lie.

"I'm not your sister's boyfriend. Why would you think that?"

His mouth is at my neck, and I can't remember why I asked the question. It's worse than an undertow, and the force of the pull makes my head spin. The warmth of his fingers on my thigh feels scandalous —indecent.

The bathing suit is not thick enough to mask the shape of his erection when he presses his hips into mine, and we both hiss at the friction.

"Stop. I'm—I need—" I need more. I have to go. "We can't do this again."

"We're bound to do this again."

"Don't say that. This kiss meant nothing."

"Nothing at all."

I'm babbling, but I can't seem to shut up. "You're obnoxious. I'm not one of your groupies. And I have a good boyfriend."

"All you're missing is a bad one." He stretches out to capture my lips again, and fuck it, I reciprocate.

I play with fire every day, but this feels more volatile and dangerous than bottling a bolt of lightning.

My nerve endings short-circuit with heat and need. A heavy fullness hovers low in my belly, and my thighs quiver. My skin tingles, my vision heightened.

He presses me harder against the rock at my back and cups my ass. All I want is to wrap my legs around him and shed the wet fabric holding us back.

I duck under his arm and stagger away.

He fights for breath, his eyes so dark that it would bring me some pride if I didn't feel so exposed.

I hold out my hands. "Stay back."

"Is that really what you want?"

From the way he asks the question, I think he will respect an inaccurate and insincere "yes," even though he knows it's crap. My tongue won't allow me to lie, so I stay silent. I thread my fingers in his hair and pull his mouth to mine one last time. He grins against the kiss but doesn't deepen it, letting me flee. But Gods, the devilish smile on his swollen lips gives me no doubt that this is merely a timeout.

I've officially gone insane. Either that or I'm spellbound. I chew on the possibility, the brush of Cole's tongue still fresh in my memory, and admit that it's probably not about magic.

It's the rivalry. The connection.

The raw need to have him pinned beneath me and make him beg, and I know he feels the same. It's a vicious, insidious thought because, while winning sounds pretty amazing, losing would be fucking incredible.

I squeeze my eyes shut, my heart beating in my throat, my bottoms soaked through.

I can't let these fantasies derail my mission.

If I sleep with him, he'll be the one hailed as a hero.

I'll be squashed like a bug and lose the respect of my friends. No guy—no silly fantasy—is worth that.

Cole gives me a head start, and I return to my friends empty handed. Lydia squeezes my shoulders. Allie eyes me suspiciously, but I avoid her inquisitive gaze.

Brie is celebrating her win with her crew. The jeweled crown rests on her head. She wiggles her brows at me and starts to sing, an old mermaid song I've heard the beat to before, but I can't quite place the lyrics.

Trent, Lydia, and Olson mutter along.

A lovely, lovely boy came to the sea
He was cold and lonely
He wanted more than the sea could give
So, he asked for oblivion instead
A lovely, lovely girl came after him
She pulled him out of the waves
She wanted his love for herself
So, she stole from the dead
When the sea came to collect its due
The girl was alone in their bed
Gone was her lover; gone was her head
For when a boy and a girl drown together
One corpse always sinks deeper
Come to the sea with no demands
Prepare yourself to make amends
Bring your lover if you wish
And watch him laugh while you perish

Trent wraps an arm around my shoulders. "Wow, that shit is depressing."

"Life is depressingly funny. We all want what we can't have," Brie chimes. She stretches both arms above her head and winks at me on her way to the beer kegs. "Especially Julia." Her hand skims the crown, but I'm not fooled. She's not talking about me losing the challenge.

My cheeks burn, my chest constricts, and my pride sinks like a stone past my feet.

She saw.

She saw it all.

33

MIRANDA

"Are you going to tell anyone?" I ask Brie the next day.

We've just suffered through our last History of Magic lesson for the quarter, and the mermaid's hair is messier than usual. It's rare that I can get a minute alone with her, but I need to know if she's going to run her mouth about what she saw. My finals start tomorrow, so it'd be the perfect time to mess with my concentration.

She looks glum as she answers, "About what?"

I click my tongue. "Don't play with me, Brie."

The hunch of her shoulders worsens before she sighs, "I have no clue what you're talking about. Now, leave me alone. I can't be seen talking to you."

I cut in front of her. "I need an answer."

She bares her teeth. "What the fuck are you harassing me for?"

I pause. My boots dig into the mud left by yet another winter drizzle. "You're serious. You don't have any idea what I'm talking about?"

"None. Please leave me alone."

Brie hurries off, and I'm left gaping at her retreating back.

She doesn't remember. There's genuine confusion behind the snark, and my arms fall at my sides. I was so sure she'd seen Cole and

195

me in the water...her song, her jab. I couldn't have read all of this wrong, could I?

Before I have a chance to really process Brie's behavior, shouts and claps catch my attention.

Bright red graffiti glistens on the roof of the dining hall.

Mortals belong on our staff, not in our schools.

I swallow hard and slow down.

A flash of blue hair turns my stomach to stone. Jessa beams from my right as she points at the hateful artwork. "I wonder who did this. I'd love to send them fan mail."

"Address it to yourself then," I snap.

"I didn't do this. I didn't need to. All the immortals are starting to realize how poisonous you are." The happiness on her face grates my indignant heart. "You should quit before anyone else gets hurt."

"You should stop hurting people."

Olson catches up to me and grabs my hand, holding me back. Jessa certainly deserves a second punch in the face, but I know that would only get her what she wants. Me, expelled.

There's a weird vibe sizzling the air, like this isn't just some other student prank. On the roof, two men in black cloaks are inspecting the graffiti.

"Is that..."

"Human blood. Yes," Olson growls.

What the—

"Julia Winslow?"

I spin around. Three Magisterium agents with identical black cloaks form a circle around me. Their appearances are intimidating as shit, and for a moment I'm frozen.

"Y-Yes?"

"Please come with us," one agent says.

Magical shackles appear around my wrist, and an invisible force pushes me along the path.

"Where are you taking me?" I ask, my voice squeaky.

Jessa eats up every bit of the moment, her smirk wider by the second.

"Come with us, Ma'am," a second agent says as the magical force field presses harder on my back. "You've been accused of poaching from the Magisterium's garden."

Blood rushes to my ears. "No. I didn't."

A hot flush covers my neck.

They guide me quickly to the administrative building. A few students we cross paths with snap pictures. The agents force me down a narrow staircase to a dark room in the back of the humid basement.

Oz is there, waiting. His shoulders are hunched, and his right brow is bent in a perfect L-shape. He doesn't meet my gaze. The disappointment on his face is so thick that I frown.

"You have the right to remain silent, Ma'am. But I would advise against it," the tallest agent says before the magic releases me.

I breathe easier knowing Oz is here and take a seat at the table between us. The Magus behind me gives me enough space to shake out my arms. "What's going on?"

Oz places a bushel of bloodroots on the table. "These were found in your dresser. I know you've been bullied. Maybe you thought this would help you get even, but it's a crime, Julia."

My mind is blank until— "I'm being set up." Bloodroots are very powerful and very rare. They take forever to dig out and can't come in contact with sunlight, and I know I didn't spend the night in the garden. "I haven't touched the garden. Someone must have put these roots in my room."

Oz shakes his head. "I checked. There was no sign of intrusion. No other heat signatures went through the door in twenty-four hours. I want to help you, Julia. But I'm going to need the truth. Did someone put you up to this?"

My mouth stings. It hurts that he doesn't believe me. I thought that I could count on Oz to see through the lies the immortals are weaving. I was wrong. "I've never seen these roots before in my life. I swear."

I search his gaze, hoping, praying he'll reconsider.

The other agents are quiet and give my professor free rein, and then it hits me. Is he a Magisterium agent? Is Oz their representative at the Academy?

A sad grimace curls his lips. "There was a very specific magic signature on it. It had to be you."

A crystalline voice resonates from behind me. "Let her go. I'm responsible for this." Miss Eillis prances into the interrogation room, her eyes fierce and her trademark skirt replaced by black leggings and a matching shirt.

"Beth?" Oz looks confused.

Miss Eillis' hair is tied into a braid, and the three agents that arrested me take a step back. "I harvested it last night and went into Julia's room this morning to comfort her. I must have misplaced it then."

"And you put them in her dresser?" Oz asks.

"I put them on the dresser, but it would have been easy enough for them to fall inside. You know your spell couldn't account for my presence there."

"Still…"

Something heavy passes between them.

"Even if Julia put them in her dresser herself after I left, she couldn't have known they belonged to the Magisterium," Miss Eillis adds. "This was all one big misunderstanding, and you guys have bigger fish to fry tonight."

Mr. Oz rests his hand on the back of the chair opposite me. "Alright."

I can tell he doesn't believe her entirely, but he sneaks glances at his colleagues and goes along with it anyway.

My mind is running laps. Bigger fish…What did that mean?

I draw in a sharp breath as Miss Eillis and I get outside after they released us. She walks so fast, I struggle to keep up. We reach Summer Hall's fair weather in record time.

"Thank you, but why did you do it? Why did you lie for me?" I ask.

"You didn't do this, but someone did. Gaïa help us. This whole school is going crazy. Everything is exactly like it was when…" She rubs the bridge of her nose. "I was here when all the mortals were found dead." She bounces her head from left to right as though she wants to shake clear an image from her mind.

My throat constricts at the dread in her voice. "You think mortals are in danger?"

She pauses for a moment and meets my gaze. "The tricky thing with wars is that they always get out of control. Mortals weren't the only ones who died that year. We're all in danger, Julia."

34

STOLEN HEARTS

The air is heavy. The sky is murky. The earth vibrates at my feet.

Miss Eillis escorts me to the dorm and doubles back in a hurry. Something big is going on. This is more than a false accusation. The agents weren't here for me.

All my witchy senses are screaming at me to run. I bite half my nails off and set up my books in the kitchen, waiting for Miss Eillis to return.

When a loud knock reverberates through the first floor, I peek through the tinted glass. Trent stands on the other side of the door, and I let out a breath of relief until I notice how ashen his skin is. His hair is wet like he just got out of the shower. The whites of his eyes are redder than usual and almost blend with his carmine irises in the darkness.

"You lied to me," he seethes.

Immediately, my back tenses. His voice is hollow and just plain wrong.

"What happened to you?" I ask gently.

"You made me think you hated him. He was nothing but horrible to you."

My mind goes blank. Did Brie tell him about Cole and me after all? I was so sure she wasn't faking her sudden memory loss, but maybe she played me.

"How can you be into Cole of all people?" There's a pause, and Trent's candor hurts more with each word because I have no good answer. His fists are balled at his sides. "I thought you were different. But you're just another Fae whore."

A boulder blocks my airways, and a shudder slices me from head to toe. A painful numbness claws its way into my stiff muscles, but I press my tongue hard against the roof of my mouth to stop the itching behind my lids. "I have nothing to say. We're over."

I swing the door to shut it in his face.

His hand shoots out to stop it. "Not before I get what I want." His glassy eyes zero in on my neck.

At first, I thought he was fighting back tears, but there's an emptiness to his gaze that clashes with his anger. It's like he's standing behind a flawed glass pane. I back away from the porch, but it's too late.

He's on me in half a second. Long fingers scratch at my shoulders.

I send him flying back with a burst of heat and run. My feet scramble to keep me from tumbling down to the glassy hardwood, and I yank the screen door open, heading toward the gardens.

The fluorescent cedar cuts into my arms as I jump behind the thick hedge, using the tall plants as cover. What the fuck is going on? Trent wasn't just mad at me about Cole. He was high, under a spell of some kind, mind control maybe, and his murderous glare left no doubt that he wanted to bite me. Ducking behind a bush, I catch my breath and listen for his footsteps.

A high-pitched scream turns my heart upside down. From the corner of my eyes, I see Blane and Bailey dragging Lydia toward their room. My pulse escalates. It's not just Trent, then.

"Here, kitty, kitty, kitty," the vampire chimes, his voice getting louder and louder.

I watch through the dark bushes and let my fire build up. If I use too much, I'll hurt him, but I can't actually wrestle him into submission either.

Holding both my hands in front of me, I steel myself and stand up. "Let's talk about this."

"No talking." He crouches forward, his arms stretched on both sides to block a possible escape.

The magic in my fingers begs for freedom, but there's got to be a way to shake him out of this trance.

"Please, Trent. Something is making you act this way," I plead.

The whiplash of his attack causes my hair to tangle in the cedar. My head spins, and I release my fire.

Teeth sink into flesh.

I scream.

The smell of burnt flesh turns my stomach, but Trent doesn't stop. He just pushes me to the ground and drinks from my open vein until his body is torn off me.

Cole tosses Trent aside violently. Dark energy pulses around him. The two struggle, but deep burns are etched into Trent's chest, and Cole looks ready to tear his head off.

"Wait! Something isn't right! He's under some kind of spell!" I shout at the blurry pair, and the mass of limbs stills for an instant.

Cole's eyes are glassy as fuck, too.

Holy hell.

The prince flattens Trent to the dirt and chokes him.

"Stop! You're going to kill him!" My nails sink deep into Cole's shoulder.

Trent gasps and staggers to his knees. Cole gives him one nasty kick in the ribs, and my crazed boyfriend bites the ground, his eyes rolling inward.

I press my hands hard on each side of Cole's face and force him to look at me. "Stop!"

"I should kill him. He wants what's mine."

The possessive adjective twists and pulls at every nerve and fills my chest with a searing heat. If Cole was in his right mind, I'd give him hell for it.

"He's unconscious. You won." I check that Trent is breathing. Kneeling beside him, I take his pulse and frown at the amount of dirt underneath his fingernails. What happened to him? What happened to them both? "We need to help Lydia. I saw Blane—"

Cole shoves me away from Trent's unconscious form. "You don't want me to finish him because you still want him."

I slip on a puddle and fall flat to my ass.

Cole's amber eyes are so dilated, they're all black, and the sinister stare flicks from me to Trent and back for a few rounds, like he's listening to my words but doesn't fully believe them. The Fae I have in front of me is not to be reasoned with, but tamed, the way you approach a wild lion.

A delicate touch and a fine piece of bargaining meat might spare me from getting eaten.

"I don't want him." I chew the insides of my cheeks hard. "I want you, Cole"

I've got his attention now.

"Say it again."

"I want you." I extend my hand for good measure.

How ironic that I can only be honest with him while he's in this state?

He climbs over me, his knee between my thighs, and I hold my breath. The dark glint in his eyes isn't erased by my admission. It melts into something far less hateful but equally wicked. "You're mine, Fire Girl."

His thumb flicks over my nipple, and my lips part in a shocked gasp. It's so unexpected and without preamble that I shudder. He's never been quite so brazen before. The weight of his body pins me down to the ground. Contrary to Trent's attack, this one is fluid and seductive.

Heartbeats resonate across my ribs, my belly. A hot, wild pulse radiates outward to the tips of my fingers and toes. I'm a beating heart in his arms, and he's going to crush me.

Fae love two things. Sex and deals.

I trace the shape of his ear. "I'll make you a deal. You help me find

Lydia, and I'll kiss you again."

"You'll kiss me regardless."

That prince. Always playing games. It's horrible that I'm turned on, bloodied, and a mere foot from Trent's unconscious body. Cole doesn't seem to be asking permission, and his fingers fumble with the buttons of my shirt.

I palm his cheek and catch his gaze again. "I know what you want. You can get it, but not now. Now, you have to help me find Lydia."

"Why shouldn't I take it now?" He asks like we're talking about an apple or a pen.

"It wouldn't be the same, and you know it." I pray that his fogged brain still understands the difference.

He stops, his fingers an inch shy of my breast. "Swear it. Formally."

"By the Dark Gods, I swear it."

He seals my promise with a kiss before he peels himself off me and offers me his hand.

With our fingers twined, I crawl to my feet.

Hysteria rises in my blood. What did I just do?

There's no time for second-guesses, so I run toward the snakes' bedroom. Cole breaks down the door with one powerful kick, and I march inside with fireballs ready to fly.

Lydia is alone in the back, tied up to the wall. Tears stream down her cheeks, but she looks in one piece.

"Jules!"

I start loosening the knots around her wrists. Cole steps behind me, his bare arms on either side of mine, and cuts the ropes with a shiny dagger.

Lydia's panic dims in the face of her rescue, her heavy breaths slow down a bit, and she slowly rubs her lower arms. "Blane and Bailey... They tied me up and started saying all sorts of crazy things. I know they're jerks, but I swear they had a dreamy glint in their eyes...like they weren't quite there."

"Trent attacked me. Fangs blazing and with nothing but hunger on his mind. Something is making them act this way. They've gone... savage," I explain.

Lydia's gaze flicks over to Cole like she's only now realizing that he's three quarters unhinged. She inches backwards. "Is he…"

"Affected? Yeah, but as it turns out, his uninhibited self is not far from his real personality. Just hornier."

With a devilish grin, Cole wraps his arm around my midriff, his heated palm curling around my throat.

Lydia's eyes bulge.

I slap the prince's hand away, but he just squeezes me to him, his fingers hard at my neck, his chest harder at my back. My train of thought is becoming blurrier by the second. "It must be a spell or something."

Cole presses his nose to my pulse point and inhales like I'm a one-man pheromone party. "It was in the food."

"Huh?"

"We all ate at the same time. Darkwood, the snake twins, and me. We'd just gotten out of detention."

"Detention? Don't you mean the immortal seminar for a more inclusive school?" I snap.

He growls. "Don't push me, Fire Girl. I'm already tired of waiting."

I comb my hair away from my face and try to get my thoughts in order. "Okay. If it was in the food, it means it's got to be a potion."

"Or a poison," Cole adds clinically.

"Given most immortals' metabolisms, it should wear out by itself pretty quickly. Shouldn't we just find a good place to hide?" Lydia offers.

I point to the dark prince of lust who's now kissing a fiery trail down my neck. "Waiting is out of the question. We need another plan."

Cole pulls on my shirt, stretches the neckline, and pushes my bra strap past the bend in my shoulder.

I've got half a mind to let him lead me into a dark corner and let him have his Fae prince way with me. With everything going on, I would have plausible deniability, but I know I wouldn't see it the same way if our roles were reversed. Whatever is happening, he's not in control.

Suddenly, he falls down on his back, and I jump in surprise.

Oz and his three sidekicks from the Magisterium enter the room. Force fields shimmer in and out of view as they hold Cole down. The Prince thrashes and curses and manages to crawl to a sitting position.

Wind blows into the room and brings a few flowers and leaves with it. Miss Eillis marches past Oz and the other men. A fresh rush of energy fills the room, and the walls shake. The white strands of hair on her head dance angrily around her body, unaffected by the powerful wind.

Cole coughs, and his head snaps back down to the ground with a loud thump.

Miss Eillis steps over him, opens his mouth and dumps a red liquid down his throat. Immediately, he stops resisting, and his body relaxes.

"It's done," she says, and the agents back off. "Let's find the others."

Cole grabs his head with both hands and groans. "Ow. What happened?"

Eillis and Oz hurry out, but one agent stays behind.

I help Cole up. "Don't you remember?"

His limbs are shaky as hell. "It's like a fuzzy dream." His mouth struggles with the choppy words, and his dazed stare bounces around like he doesn't quite know who I am or how he got here.

When his eyes focus on our joined hands, he suddenly pulls away.

He doesn't mention our deal, and I wonder if it stands even though he forgot about it. Is the magic still there?

Do I really owe Cole my virginity? Or was the phrasing dubious enough to save me?

The Magisterium agent leads Cole out of Summer Hall, and I follow, stunned. A crowd has formed out front. Another five or so agents set a barrier to keep people away from my dorm. I find Allie and Olson in the mayhem and hurry toward them.

My sister hugs me tight. "When they said there'd been an attack, I thought…" Her eyes widen at the bloody spots on my neck and my chafed arms, but it's the scars she can't see that bother me the most.

"I'm okay."

Trent, Cole, Blane, and Bailey walk with their heads down to the main office under the watchful eyes of Professor Oz and Miss Eillis.

"Looks like a few immortals are going to miss their finals," Olson says with a dark laugh.

Something eerie lingers in his body language, in the evil curve of his mouth, and in the "just desserts" tone of his voice...

It gnaws at me, and I jerk around to face him. My blood runs at the satisfied smirk on his lips.

Without thought, I push the warlock square in the chest. "You did this? We almost got killed!"

He shakes me off and stands tall. "Hey, I had to do something. They were going to send us home and brush this whole thing under the rug. Act like we were the ones falling behind, not being constantly bullied and attacked by those beasts."

With both fists curled at my sides, I raise a brow. "And what did this stunt prove?"

"That we can survive anything. And that their killer instincts that they hold in such high regard are actually their biggest liability." There's no remorse on his face. Only righteous anger.

"You're insane."

He shakes his head from side to side. "Wake up, Jules. They're never going to give us equality. We have to take it. The end justifies the means."

"You targeted immortals that have a direct link to me. Why?" My troubled boyfriend, my nemesis, and my house mates. That can't be a coincidence.

He shrugs. "Bad luck, I'm afraid. They were all in detention together."

I can't shake the feeling that this was targeted at me, somehow. Olson must have had help. If he wasn't the one who wanted to hurt me, who was? "Why was Trent in detention?" I ask, still trying to piece out the puzzle.

Olson shrugs. "Something to do with missing curfew last night. I heard he didn't return until dawn."

My heart sinks.

He missed curfew. Dirt soiled his nails. No heat signature went in and out of my room in the last twenty-four hours even though I was framed for a crime I didn't commit.

I think I found my bloodroot thief.

35

TRUTH AND DARE

"What are you doing here, Trent?" My hand firmly holds Summer Hall's front door.

I've just finished my exams for the day, and the last thing I need is a repeat from yesterday's drama. I don't resent Trent for Olson's actions, but there is no doubt in my mind that he's the one who tried to frame me for the bloodroot theft. And while I understand he was enchanted to act like a murderous maniac, the memories from last night aren't quite that easy to brush off.

The vampire looks taken aback by the steel in my voice. His brown hair is oily, and he hasn't shaved in a few days. "They insisted I come. To officially apologize."

I cross my arms over my chest. "For biting me or for setting me up?"

His shoulders sag with a sense of complete abdication. "I'm sorry, Jules."

My hand flies to my forehead. "You know what, I don't even want to hear your reasons. You are the worst of them. You pretended to care about me only to stab me in the back."

"You'd be safer elsewhere," he says with a wince.

A dry snicker dies on my lips. "You want me to believe you care about my safety?"

A shadow passes over his haunted face. "Clearly, you don't."

"Clearly."

He turns on his heels, his fists balled at his sides, but he stops cold at the top of the porch's stairs. "You're not the first Winslow to spread your legs for him, you know."

I flip him off.

"Your sister is no better. She had her tongue down Cole's throat in record time on Halloween. They giggled their way up the North path and never looked back. I should have known he'd want to perfect his score card, but I can't wrap my mind around why she hasn't told you."

"You're lying," I croak, thinking he's just trying to spook me.

"You can see for yourself." He offers me his hand, his tongue tucked under his right canine. He scratches a bloody line in his neck and raises a brow.

"You must think I'm an idiot." I want to slam the door in his face and not look back. But if he's telling the truth, I need to know. If he could shed some light on the mystery of what happened to Allie on Halloween, I can't turn my back on the opportunity.

"There's no other way to do this. You drink my blood; I drink yours."

A shudder runs through me when I lick the droplets on his neck. He tastes coppery but sweet, and my mouth waters for more. I gather my thick mane to the side and bare my neck. "Do it. Show me everything you remember."

The puncture wounds from yesterday are still fresh, and I bite back a groan of pain.

Images flash behind my lids as Trent takes me through his memories from Halloween.

Allie is dressed to impress, wearing a cute black cat costume, her blouse tied underneath her breasts. She's hanging with Mel by the kegs when Flynn hops over to her.

"Hey, Allie. Serve us a glass," the Fae asks, drinking in Mel's cleavage in the process.

Allie pours the beer for Flynn and Cole. I can practically see her shaking.

Flynn snatches her wrist and pulls her forward to the bonfire. "Come and sit with us."

Mel rolls her eyes and stomps off.

The evening flashes forward to later.

Trent takes a sip of wine and stumbles up the winding path leading away from the beach. He's piss drunk, so his vision is a bit blurred. Brie is by his side, helping him along.

Giggles rise from behind a big rock, and he peeks at the happy couple.

The sight of my sister kissing Cole stops my heart. Her hands dig inside Cole's hair. She's got him pinned against the rock but stops as Trent comes closer.

"Your taste in women is going downhill, Desirys," Brie cracks.

Cole flips her off and twines his fingers with Allie's. "Come on, Sabrina. Let's find somewhere more private." Cole ushers my sister away.

She gives Trent and Brie a long, long look before she follows Cole into the darkness.

My insides turn to stones.

I curse myself for believing him. How could I let my guard down around a manipulative Fae prince?

Stupid.

Naive.

Fucking idiot.

"WE BETTER ACE THIS TEST, or we'll both lose the bet," I say to Cole on the morning of the S&S final. My hands shake. I want to scream at him, but that's the surest way to flunk this class.

Cole's mother arranged everything so the three immortal victims of Olson's hardcore prank won't be penalized by the events of last week. They won't miss their exams after all.

The prince's stool winces under his weight as he sits next to me. The skin on his face is slightly gray and dark circles lurk under his eyes, but he looks more like himself than he did last time I saw him.

"Let's concentrate on the task at hand. We can talk after," the lying fiend answers.

After three grueling hours of teamwork, Deveraux pulls names out of the hat one by one and evaluates our latest spells at our tables. Potions, vials, and cauldrons send a nefarious smog into the air. My eyes water from the volatile stink. Cole raps his fingers on the desk, but I refuse to meet the prince's gaze until Deveraux grades our spell.

By some twist of fate, we're the only two left in the classroom by the time Deveraux walks over to us.

She wets the tip of her feather with her lips. "You chose a difficult, unstable spell. I hope you didn't let your little feud run you out of my class."

Cole and I exchange a glance. Sweat gathers at the nape of my neck. The Fae hands Deveraux the bulb-shaped bottle and clenches his leather bag.

The teacher examines the color and turbidity of the liquid. "A bit too clear, but acceptable shade." She uncorks the bottle and uses a small pipette to suck a few drops out. She deposits one over her finger and rolls the elixir between her index and thumb. "Nice texture."

She walks over to the empty space in front of the class and throws the vial in the potted plant in the corner. The frail glass breaks on impact, and I hold my breath. Smoke rises in the air and condenses above the hibiscus bush. A small lightning bolt illuminates the ceiling, and rain starts to pour down on the leaves.

Deveraux scribbles a few words in her notebook. The artificial cloud grumbles but stops after a minute, content that the plant below is correctly nourished.

Cole and I both sigh in relief.

A smile curls Deveraux's serious scowl. "Summoning a stable, portable cloud is a tremendous skill. I hope this proves you work better together than against each other." She snaps her notebook shut. "Prepare yourselves for next quarter. Winter is my favorite moon season." With that, she hustles out of class.

My eyes widen when Cole grabs the leg of the stool that's directly between my legs and pulls me closer to him. He leans over me and whispers, "Don't act weird." He nudges my side. "You spent the whole morning at the edge of the desk like I have the plague or something."

"You are the plague."

His back stiffens. "Aren't you glad you didn't fuck him?" His voice comes out gruff.

I grit my teeth hard enough for them to chip.

Cole crosses his arm. "Darkwood hates me. Doesn't mean he's not on my side. Every immortal is on my side."

"You erased Brie's memory," I say, thinking it makes the most sense.

"I slightly altered her recollection of the beach games. She was going to run her mouth about us. I thought you'd be grateful."

I jump to my feet and walk to the magic slime disposal in the back to clean my cauldron. "Why would it be so bad for you? It was just a stupid kiss."

Cole's hands are tight around his cauldron's handle as he joins me by the big bronze tub. Magic slime slowly drools into the drain. "Don't you remember the part about my mother banishing me to Faerie?"

He's making sense. Fury pumps through my veins and warms up my blood into an inferno. The ends of my hairs shimmer with flames, and I scrub the tin interior of my cauldron vigorously with the special brush. "It's not just Brie. You lied about Allie."

His hand pauses on the faucet. "Did I?"

I dump everything into the bottom of the tub and turn to Cole. "You're fucking her and messing with her head. I saw you leading her away in Trent's memory. You've had her under your spell since Halloween."

"Then I guess it must be true." He raises his palms nonchalantly, but his eyes are dark, and he walks away with his half-clean cauldron.

"This is all a big game to you. Seducing my sister. Seducing me. What? You figured we would make great notches on Cole Desirys' golden bedpost?"

"Don't flatter yourself." He shoves his things in his bag in a hurry.

Hands on my hips, I follow him. "Just admit it. I need to know what happened that night. It's not like you would get in trouble for it, so just brag about it to me like I'm sure you did to your buddies."

He averts his gaze, his eyes to the ceiling, and wraps his jacket around his frame. "I got piss drunk on Halloween and passed out. I'd love to play the villain in every one of your faux-dramas, but I didn't touch your sister."

"Stop lying! I saw it with my own eyes!"

He almost runs out of the classroom, and the urgency in his movements throws me for a loop. I thought he'd gloat, but this isn't the face of a guy who's happy showing off his conquests.

This is the face of a man who has something to hide.

CAT GOT YOUR TONGUE

as soon as Cole steps out of the main building, he bee-lines toward the forest. I wait for him to disappear and follow. My breaths and footsteps are muffled by a silence spell, but I still almost lose him in the cold evening. The fog places itself exactly where he needs it, and the birds are quiet on his path.

The deeper I get into the woods, the more certain I am that this isn't about Allie. Something I said spooked him, but I don't know exactly what.

The hike is steep and involves a lot of back and forth like he's effectively trying to muddle his trail.

When I get to a meadow on the north side of the Fall's cliffs, a thick shadow stands in front of me, not unlike the one that chased me down to the falls party. It hisses, and its tendrils lick my skin.

Instead of running scared, I examine the apparition.

The shadow resembles a black mirror. It hangs in mid-air, almost like a portal, and I push a bit of infernal magic forward. There's enough light to glimpse its edges. The shadow purrs, and a thousand black orbs of smoke arrange into the form of a cat.

Like I've suddenly stepped through glass, the woods around me are no longer foggy. A big black tiger with reflective blue irises and hirsute fur scratches its side against a tree.

Cole pets the tiger's head with a sigh. "I knew you were fearless. I didn't know you were stupid."

My nostrils flare, and I let my powers build. Fire expands and pools in my cells. "You have a demon familiar."

It explains everything. The raven. The shadow. The attacks. Cole hasn't been doing all that by himself. He's had help.

Holly. Lydia. Cole is at the root of the cancer festering in Dark Falls.

"Yes. She's beautiful, isn't she?" His amiable features are wiped away by a calculated glare. It feels as though he's actually asking.

I curl my hands into fists. He's playing with me, taunting me, and I won't give him the satisfaction. "Allie's not a mean, hare-brained girl. I don't know how you did it, how you got her under your spell, but I'll find out what you did to her and when I do…"

"Will you let me talk?"

And I hate myself, because I want to hear what he has to say. I want to know why, but most of all, my heart is weeping for a reasonable explanation.

"It was you all along. The beast. The shadow. You summoned that demon to slaughter us all."

His lips press in a hard line.

All my hopes that this might not be as dire as I think are erased by the cruel curve of his mouth. "Mortals shouldn't be allowed here."

The vindication nearly floors me.

I arch a sarcastic brow. "Even me?"

"Especially you." The word resonates like an ominous choir you'd hear in a dark satanic ritual. "Onyx here isn't meant to kill. She's here to drive some much-needed self-preservation into your lot. If you stay, you'll become a bigger and bigger target until someone decides to slit your throats while you sleep. Haven't you heard the stories?" He stalks toward me like I'm the one being unreasonable. Like he's doing me a favor.

He reaches for my hand, but I push my arms forward and aim every bit of magic I possess straight at his chest.

His tall frame is blasted a hundred feet back. The recoil from the explosion burns my clothes, and a grunt of pain passes through my tight lips.

Strips of melted fabric fall off his tattooed chest as Cole stands. Blue and black Fae magic spills from his fingers, and his beast rattles at his side. "Is that all you got?"

And so, I run.

If he erased Brie's memory and toyed with Allie, I don't want to find out what he'll do to me.

I cut myself on a rock. The red and black plaid is burnt to a crisp, and my thighs are tainted with charcoal streaks.

The tips of my toes curl around the edge of the cliff. A salty breeze bellows from the sea. Dark waves crash against the rocks below, their stormy roils sounding like thunderous applause to my demise.

He prowls up the path. His pale skin catches the moonlight, and the uneven thumps in my chest terrify me more than the cold glint burning in his eyes.

Sickening tingles scatter across my neck.

His gaze softens for a split second. "Kneel, Fire Girl."

The coastal wind blows my hair forward. The long dark strands undulate like snakes at the edge of my vision. "Never."

He wraps his hand in my hair with a tenderness that devours my heart.

What twisted game is this? Whatever it is, I feel like I'm losing.

He crushes his mouth to mine like he did the first time. With one kiss, he steals my voice and my resolve. I don't know anything for sure anymore, just that Cole Desirys is my enemy. I can't trust one word coming out of his sinful mouth, but I can't get enough of him.

Maybe I should start focusing on how he cursed me.

Because this crush, this plague, this abominable, needy hole in my chest...

It can't be real.

I cling to that belief with both hands, desperate to hang on to a smidgen of self-respect.

My heartbeat pulses in my throat, and I find solace in the knowledge that I might not be entirely to blame for this dark addiction.

In a minute, I'll find the strength to shove him off me. I'll untangle this mess and get revenge. I'll get the answers I so desperately crave.

Slowly, almost regretfully, he inches away. His hands fall from my hair to my shoulders and caress my skin. The languid brush of his fingers unravels the threads of my soul in such a way that I don't know if I can trust my own thoughts anymore. His chest heaves, his breaths come out in rasps, and his mouth is swollen from the intensity of our kiss.

"The raven who crashed into the window...the one who led me to your hideout...it was you," I surmise.

"Yes."

"You've been lying this whole time."

"Barely." He shakes his head like I'm being silly. "And you're not going to tell anyone about me."

"Because you cursed me," I say, thinking he's finally admitting that I'm under his quite literal spell.

His cunning gaze pierces into mine. "Because you can't afford for anyone to know I have a thing for demons."

The threat is crystal clear, and my eyes widen.

"Don't worry, your scandalous little secret is safe with me."

"I'll tell them anyway," I bluff.

"No, you won't. You want to be here as much as I need you gone." The haunted tremble of his voice is not fabricated, and he leans close enough for his nose to brush mine.

The soft touch fractures my poker face. "What's the plan? You get us out one by one?"

"I'd hoped, after Holly, that you and your people would come to your senses."

My voice breaks with hatred. "Then you chose Lydia."

"Lydia saw Onyx in the woods. She's a clever girl. Onyx did what she had to do," he whispers, and for the first time, his voice betrays a smidgen of unease. He cradles my hand in his.

I want to shove him off, but he's talking, so I humor him. "What about Allie?"

"Allie is a complication. Something big happened here on Halloween, and your sister is at the crux of the mystery. I wasn't lying about her. I have no idea who she's been seeing, but it's certainly not me."

Worst part is: I think I believe him. Tears flood my eyes, but I swallow the salty sting. He's telling me everything. That can only mean he plans to silence me forever. "If you're going to try and kill me, just do it already."

His hand closes around the nape of my neck. "What a waste that would be. I might not remember what happened on Halloween, but I haven't forgotten our deal."

The tight hold makes my head spin, and my entrails do a triple somersault. "Err—"

He caresses the side of my face as though I'm the most precious jewel in his collection, but his fingers dig viciously into my waist. "You know the drill. A deal with a Fae is unbreakable, and you've promised. Now, you're going to add to that promise and vow not to share what you saw, what I said, or your suspicions in general in any way, shape, or form."

Each heartbeat pulses inside my chest harder than the last. Boom.

Boom.

Boom.

This is the only way out, at least for now.

Dread fills my mouth, but I utter the words he needs to hear. "I swear it."

He nods solemnly and takes a step back.

"Wait. About...the other thing. You promised to wait," I whisper, my mouth dry.

He presses his lips to mine for a second before his trademark grin curls his lips. A sinister gleam dances in his eyes. "I didn't say how long."

I stand there, half-burnt in both senses of the word, until his silhouette disappears from view.

How did I end up here? I betrayed every promise I've made to myself.

Whatever magic Cole has been weaving, I can dispel it and have his ass booted back to Faerie. I can find a way around this deal and protect my secret. When I do, everything will go back to normal, and this wretched feeling in my chest will disappear.

If it doesn't, it means I've fallen for a wicked prince.

CHEATED

"*T*he top three students this quarter are: Cole Desirys, Melanie Darkwood, and Julia Winslow." Celeste Draco's voice ices over my name. "Please join me up here."

Applauses resonate around the auditorium. It's the Saturday before the Uranis break. In ten days, a new quarter begins. The stage is flanked by red velvet curtains, and the polished wood of the stage gleams under the spotlight.

The moment of truth.

Cole's back is to me. He's sitting to my left, several rows forward, and straightens his jacket before walking up the red carpet. A few students shout his name.

I join him and Melanie on stage. Cole's proximity creates an uncomfortable itch that runs from the back of my hand to the tip of my ear.

Deveraux takes the podium and delivers a heartfelt speech about inclusion and how we must all strive to bridge our differences and come together in the new quarter to come. She invites us to shed our anger and mend fences.

When she glances into the winner's envelope, my back stiffens. Cole shoots me a condescending glare like he already knows he's won.

Maybe he does know, and my confidence fizzles. I remind myself I don't have to win to stay at the Academy. I only have to beat Cole.

If Melanie takes this, we'll have to wait for the report cards to be handed out after the ceremony.

"Dark Falls' best student for the Saturnalia quarter is...Julia Winslow."

Surprised gasps and tame applause are quickly drowned out by Flynn's scream.

"That's bullshit," the blond Fae shouts, his voice hard as steel.

"Enough, Verinos," Mr. Oz says from the sidelines.

"No! She might have aced S&S, but there's no way she got an A in Divination after the stunt she pulled. And Cole got an A in everything."

"The report cards are still in Wright's hands," Melanie barks.

Flynn sneers. "His mother runs this school. You think he hasn't seen his yet? You bloody fool."

Oz grabs his arm, but the Fae shakes him off and points an accusing finger at me. "You cheated. I don't know how, but you did. I'm going to ruin you, Winslow."

"Come with me. Now," Oz says.

Mr. Brady moves to help him, and Flynn is dragged out of the room. Celeste hurries after them. Students whisper between themselves, and a few murderous glances latch onto me.

I swallow hard.

Deveraux shakes her head from side to side like she's completely discouraged. "Go now, and use the time off to reflect on yourselves. Magic is not the only important skill one must master." She squares the papers in her hands and motions for the crowd to disperse.

Melanie turns to me. "Congrats. I might not be okay with you dating my brother, but beating Cole is an accomplishment."

"Thanks." I'm too surprised to think of a jab, and she walks away.

Cole and I are the only ones left on the stage.

I raise my gaze to meet his. "You were fierce competition. I'm not going to rub your nose in it."

"You cheated." The words are quiet. Deadly.

My mouth opens in outrage. "I did not. We had a deal, you know. You have to uphold your end of the bargain now. All mortals should be safe from you and your tricks."

A low growl rumbles at the back of his throat, his face livid, his fists tucked deep into his jacket's pockets. "Nothing is settled."

He walks off, and I stare for a good minute at his retreating back.

What Flynn said gnaws at me. I'm not too worried about the Divination exam because Lydia helped me, but Miss Eillis let it slip that I got A- in Herbology. If Flynn wasn't lying, and Cole got an A in everything, it means I should have lost.

On the way out, I grab my report card from Mr Wright and tear it open. A slow, shaky breath flies out of me.

Oz is chatting with Mr. Brady by the exit.

"You gave me an A+ in Duel?" I ask him with a smile.

The dashing professor excuses himself from his conversation and leads me to the corner of the auditorium. "You deserved it. You sent my best fighter into a half-day magical coma. It took three healers to wake him."

Heat blossoms on my cheek, and I tuck a strand of hair behind my ear. "But that's bad. I used forbidden magic."

Oz cracks a smile and leans closer. "Maybe, but let me let you in on a little secret. Duel isn't about rules. It's about sniffing out the best warriors, so we can turn them into the most powerful Magus the world has ever seen. Your enemies in the real world will not obey a stupid student handbook to keep things fair. I stand by my grade."

Warmth and excitement foam into little bubbles of joy in my belly. "Thank you."

"You earned it, Jules." His wide grin sends my blood flying.

Oz believes in me.

With him in my corner, I'll show them all that I deserved this win and take the prize again next quarter.

I'll show all of them I didn't cheat.

I won't let a stupid prince distract me from my goals.

I will find a way to out Cole as the psychopath that he is and pry Allie from his influence. Yes, I'll slay my demon next quarter, even if I have to give my life for it.

Jules' story continues in Wicked Prince.